The Enchanted

The first book from the internationally bestselling author Rene Denfeld, *The Enchanted* is a wondrous and redemptive novel told from the point of view of a convict, whose magical interpretations of prison life allow him to find absolute joy while isolated from the rest of humanity, and a female investigator, who experiences her own personal salvation in her work as a death penalty investigator. Lyrical and heartwarming, *The Enchanted* is about the humanity that can lie within what is monstrous and the human capacity to transcend and survive.

HARPER PERENNIAL OLIVE EDITIONS

This book is part of a special series from Harper Perennial called Olive Editions—exclusive small-format editions of some of our bestselling and celebrated titles, featuring beautiful and unique hand-drawn cover illustrations. All Olive Editions are available for a limited time only.

"An amazing read. The writing is worth underlining about every other sentence."
—Annie, Bank Square Books, Mystic, Connecticut

"A debut novel from a seasoned journalist and death penalty investigator, *The Enchanted* is all tone and mood, intimations and metaphor. There is so much darkness here, from the death row dungeon setting to the gradual revealing of long-buried abuse and neglect, to the present-day struggles of characters both inside and outside the prison walls. And yet the novel is completely riveting, unexpectedly uplifting, startlingly beautiful, and so very worth your time."
—Kristen, Book Bug, Kalamazoo, Michigan

"I was mesmerized by *Enchanted*. I thought it read like *The Road* or *Old Man and the Sea*, very watery and without edges. . . . Denfeld's story, her arcs of character, all played out authentically."
—Carol, Northshire Bookstore, Sarasota Springs, Vermont

ALSO BY RENE DENFELD

The Butterfly Girl
The Child Finder

The Enchanted

A Novel

Rene Denfeld

HarperCollins books may be purchased for educational, business, or sales promotional use. For information please e-mail the Special Markets Department at SPsales@harpercollins.com.

FIRST HARPER PERENNIAL EDITION PUBLISHED 2015.

FIRST HARPER PERENNIAL OLIVE EDITION PUBLISHED 2020.

ISBN 978-0-06-303669-7 (Olive edition)

20 21 22 23 24   LSC   10 9 8 7 6 5 4 3 2 1

For Marty

The Enchanted

This is an enchanted place. Others don't see it but I do.

I see every cinder block, every hallway and doorway. I see the doorways that lead to the secret stairs and the stairs that take you into stone towers and the towers that take you to windows and the windows that open to wide, clear air. I see the chamber where the cloudy medical vines snake across the floor, empty and waiting for the warden's finger to press the red buttons. I see the secret basement warrens where rusted cans hide the urns of the dead and the urns spill their ashes across the floor until the floods come off the river to wash the ashes outside to feed the soil under the grasses, which wave to the sky. I see the soft-tufted night birds as they drop from the heavens. I see the golden horses as they run deep under the earth, heat flowing like molten metal from their backs. I see where the small men hide with their tiny hammers, and how the flibber-gibbets dance while the oven slowly ticks.

The most wonderful enchanted things happen here—the most enchanted things you can imagine. I want to tell you while I still have time, before they close the black curtain and I take my final bow.

I hear them, the fallen priest and the lady. Their footsteps sound like the soft hush of rain over the stone floors. They have been talking, low and soft, their voices sliding like a river current that stops outside my cell. When I hear them talk, I think of rain and water and crystal-clear rivers, and when I hear them pause, it is like the cascade of water over falls.

They are so aware of each other, they don't need to speak in complete sentences.

"Heading now?" he asks.

"Room," she says.

"Hard."

"Aren't they all?" Again I hear the rain in her voice.

The lady hasn't lost it yet—the sound of freedom. When she laughs, you can hear the wind in the trees and the splash of water hitting pavement. You can sense the gentle caress of rain on your face and how laughter sounds in the open air, all the things those of us in this dungeon can never feel.

The fallen priest can hear those things in her voice, too. That's what makes him afraid of her. Where can that freedom lead? Nowhere good, his pounding heart says.

"Which one?" he asks.

The lady is one of the few who call us by our names. She says her new client's name. It drops like a gem from her mouth. She has no idea how precious it sounds.

"York." The man in the cell next to mine.

The other men on the row say his mother named him for a slave who traveled with Lewis and Clark, or after his royal English father from some fabled city overseas—only in prison can you get away with a lie that big.

York knows the truth doesn't matter in here. Inside, the lies you tell become the person you become. On the outside, sun and reality shrink people back to their actual size. In here, people grow into their shadows.

I press my face against the crumbling wall. The soft rocks absorb their voices, but I have learned how to listen. I pick their words off the moss and stone.

He is warning her that this case, above all others, will be tough.

"Ready and prepared," I hear him say.

"Soon?" the lady asks.

I can hear the pleading in her voice. How can he not hear it? But he doesn't. He is too busy being scared of her.

The fallen priest doesn't hear the whipping in his own voice when he talks to the lady. He doesn't hear the longing and desire. He doesn't feel the wonderful wildness of the world. Though he lives inside this enchanted place, he doesn't see the enchantment in the lady; he doesn't see the enchantment in here or anywhere.

For me, being taken to this dungeon was like landing in sanctuary. For the priest, it was worse than exile. He came here not long ago, with his face dejected and the fluorescent lights shining on his thinning hair, the wrinkles drying around his eyes.

This place freezes you. Then one day they thaw you out and take you to the back of Cellblock H, and you are dead.

"Catch you later," he says.

I drop my head from the wall.

The lady walks past my cell. I slide along the cell wall toward the bars, careful not to let her see me. If she turns, I will jump on my cot and hide under the blanket. Instead, she keeps walking.

I creep closer to the bars to watch her walk. I catch a triangle of shirt at the bottom of her narrow back, the back of her heel. I have become practiced at this game, so sometimes I catch more: a tendril of shining black hair, a glimpse of a seashell ear.

I listen carefully as her footsteps recede down the row, savoring each tiny, muffled clop, saving it for later.

The fallen priest is also there, on the other side of my cell, watching her go. Slowly, he turns and walks the other way. His footsteps sound leaden. An inmate calls to him—that would be Striker, on my other side—and the priest moves reluctantly to the cell bars, ready words of comfort on his lips. He has sweat under his oxford shirt from talking to the lady. Sweat rolls down his calf and falls from his bare ankle under his loafers to the porous stone. It seeps down below to the underground caverns where the golden horses run, but no one sees.

The lady doesn't look back at the fallen priest. She strides away, her back straight and firm. She thinks of the priest and twitches the thoughts away. She needs a clear mind for meeting her new client.

The men watch her pass silently. No one catcalls the lady.

At the far end of the hall, a narrow set of ancient

stairs rises out of the gloom. We are buried here in the dungeon, deep under the cellblocks above. The cells here have never seen sunlight, and the light-bulbs in the stairwells are old and flickering.

The tight dungeonlike stairs are dark corners and spittle-drying places that a wise man avoids. The lady takes a deep breath and plunges up them. Claustrophobia has always plagued her. It has taken her years to get used to entering this prison, with its loud slamming gates and shocking claps of metal locks and her own deep memories of knowing what it is like to feel trapped. She got over her fears in the way she gets over everything—she pretends they don't exist.

Still, the stairs in our prison disturb her. Once she happened to glance up at the wall and saw a torn fingernail dangling from a crack in the stone. She knows about the crimes that take place in our enchanted place; the brutal acts that the outside never hears about, the gougings and rapes and killings. She knows these crimes occur not just against inmates but against guards and people like her.

The stairs are so old, they slope at the middle. The stone is porous and absorbs blood. It is true, ancient lettings have left pink stains. The stains have soaked into the margins of the old stones, the lady thinks.

She gets to the top of the landing and lets out a sigh of relief. The door leads down a silent hallway. Now she is at least on the ground floor. She turns down another narrow hall and climbs another short, steep set of stairs.

There, finally, at the top of an old alcove, is the room they call the Library of the Guards.

It is a large open room lined with shelf after shelf of huge ancient leather books. These are the ledgers of the dead, kept back before the days of computers. The guards sometimes pull down the old ledgers for visitors, to show them the archaic names and the spidery writing. A great-uncle of mine is in one ledger, though I would never openly admit to that. Elbert James Knowles, the faint handwriting says, and the date of his death. My own death, I figure, will be written in invisible ink, wound into the secret channels of the walls, where the little men climb with their hammers. Of computers I cannot say. I have never seen one.

In the middle of the Library of the Guards is an old scratched desk. A guard sits bleakly in the too small chair. He is large and looks heavy with discomfort. He is having his meal break. He eats from the blue regulation lunch box that all the guards carry, with an accordion lid and sections that can be flipped open easily to search for contraband. Ev-

ery now and then they bring in a drug dog to sniff
the lunches, though really, there is no way to stop
contraband altogether, at least not in this prison,
where the temptations are great, the stress is high,
and corruption is common. When a guard can sell a
pack of smokes for a hundred dollars inside, you bet
the temptation is there.

The guard waves at the lady with a handful of
squished sandwich. She is free to enter the door at
the far end of the room.

Inside this door is the death row visiting room.
The death row inmates jokingly call it the parole
room.

The death row visiting room is small. There is
a beautiful old yellow glass fixture on the ceiling—
not just a bulb in a metal cage but a real glass fixture
that throws a warm light. There is a real wood table,
too, and you can pretend it smells faintly of lemon
even if you know that no one here cleans with anything beyond sudsy gray water.

The important part is the window on the far
wall. If the inmates strain hard, they can see the sky
through that window. The clouds might be fluffy
and white one day, traced with pink and mauve the
next, or lit on fire from a sunset.

The window is the reason the death row inmates
go to the visiting room to see their lawyers and in-

vestigators. The lawyers think their clients want to see them. No, they want to see the window. When the visit ends and they are led in chains back to the dungeon underground, where they spend their days trapped in a six-by-nine cell with no window and no fresh air, a flat cot and open toilet with an endless circle of dark brown in the bowl and a flickering lightbulb in a metal cage, they can remember that scrap of sky. They might go months down in the dungeon between visits, even years. But on those rare days when they are summoned to the visiting room, they know they will see the sky.

When they return to the dungeon, they can tell the others. "It was reddish today, and the clouds were the color of plums," they might say. Or "I saw a bird—so pretty." No one will dispute them. There are some things people lie about in here—okay, people lie about most things in here. But there is one thing on death row that no one lies about, and that is what they saw in those scraps of sky.

York is already in the cage, waiting for the lady.

The cage is just big enough to hold one man. It stands nine feet tall and is made of lathe-carved wooden bars as hard as iron. Back in the early 1800s, a company in Louisiana called Dugdemona Holdings made these cages from wood they imported from Africa on the slave ships. The slaves made the cages and sometimes died in them. The cages were sold to small towns where jailers needed a place to hold the ranting or insane, and to plantations where owners needed a holding cell for runaways. The Dugdemona cages became popular with correction officers and revolutionaries, as cells for prisoners and for torture. More than one man has died of starvation in a Dugdemona cage.

There are only a handful of these famous cages left in the country. One is in our enchanted place, and it is used to hold the death row inmates for their professional visits. This is where York waits for the lady.

The lady sits in the single chair facing the cage. Her movements are deliberate and relaxed.

The lady and York study each other.

York's eyes are dark and oblong, like a bird of prey's. He has high cheekbones set in a thin face, a narrow skull capped with thin dark hair. Despite the years underground, his skin has a high, resinous color. Usually, the men who work with the lady look bleached by years spent living under the earth. The white men turn a strange translucent shade, like clear jelly, and the black men turn the sad color of eggplant. York has retained color, as if in defiance.

The lady sees York is a small man, bent and oddly formed, as if his bones grew funny. Even in the cage, he holds himself with a sense of contained force.

His ankles are chained above his paper slippers. A heavy bull chain is attached to one ankle cuff, and the bull chain threads back between the wood bars to a huge bolt embedded in the stone wall. The bull chain is in case he tries any funny business. The funny business never ends up very funny, I have noticed.

The lady sees that York's front teeth are oddly notched with a strange little groove in the middle— as if God, or the devil, wanted to fork him. These notched teeth are surprisingly clean. He brushes them three times a day, he will tell anyone with his monkey grimace. He flosses with bits of thread he pulls from the cover on his cot. Four hundred count, he chortles to anyone who is listening outside his cell door. York keeps up a constant litany on the row. Sometimes he will repeat the same soliloquy for days, until the guards swear they will go mad for listening, and then he will retreat inside his cell and stare at his hands.

York likes to think about what other people are thinking. He believes it gives him an edge. He says that twelve years on the row have honed his psychic abilities, but then, he claims, he was always psychic. Just as a blind man learns to smell better, York says his life has helped him read minds. The intense deprivation of our dungeon, he says, has made him better at what he does best: getting inside your head.

Of course, when he says this, the guards roll their eyes and comment that the only head York gets inside is his own.

Right now York believes the lady is thinking about him. He thinks she is feeling sorry for him, her poor new client who has spent twelve years waiting for death.

The lady isn't thinking that at all. She isn't even thinking about York. She is wondering how bad the roads will be on the way home. The spring weather has been fickle, and floods might close the single road leading away from our enchanted place. If that happens, she will have to stay overnight at the nearest motel, with its clanking radiators and mildew smell. Her mind is disconnected from her new client. It works better for her this way. She hasn't even brought a notebook to the interview.

The lady smiles at York and relaxes into her chair. She has been on her feet all day, and sitting is a treat. The window shows the sky is full of dark rain clouds, as dark as slate. The yellow light fixture above them is warm.

In a prison full of liars, the lady has the advantage of being completely authentic. Even a man like

York—especially a man like York—can see there is no game in her smile. There is warmth and kindness and something that looks like steel. You can tell me anything, her eyes say, because I will see the beauty in everything you say.

Eventually, York has to say something, anything, has to make his mouth move and ease the friction from his throat. The words tumble out as rough as rocks, but they are soon worn smooth, and more and more he hears himself talking—blessed surcease, a person just to *listen* to me—and the vowels round and the consonants grow into planets that become the universe that expands in the light in her dark eyes. She hears me, he thinks wildly—she *hears* me.

York talks and talks until his words sound like poetry even to him. He tells her why he has volunteered to die. "It isn't just that it is torture," he says, "being locked in a cage. It's never being allowed to touch anyone or go outside or breathe fresh air. I'd like to feel the sun again just once."

Her eyes show a sudden distance. What he said is true, but it isn't true enough.

"Okay. I'm tired of being meaningless," he admits. "I'm done, okay?"

He talks about the confused mess inside of him. He says everyone thinks sociopaths are super-smart criminals, but he is just a messed-up guy who doesn't know why he does what he does. Except there is like a switch in him, and when the switch flips on, he cannot stop.

"If it made sense, I would tell you," he says. "When you kill people, it is supposed to make sense. But it doesn't. It never does."

The lady nods. She understands.

With each secret he tells her, her eyes get darker and more satisfied. York can see from the precious slot of window that the rain clouds have lifted and the sky itself is dark. He has been speaking *forever*; he has told her secrets he has been afraid to tell anyone, secrets he suspects she knew all the time.

The look in her eyes is of a person who drank from the end of a gun barrel and found it delicious. Her eyes are filled with a strange sort of wondrous sadness, as if marveling at all the beauty and pain in the world.

She stands up. For the first time he notices how tiny she is. She looks like a little dark-haired sparrow. Her equally dark, oblong bird eyes could be his eyes, her narrow skull his own. But her bones are long and finely made, while his are crooked and bent.

She raises her hand in a gesture that looks like goodbye but also says yes.

He lifts his hand cautiously. His fingers are thin from lack of use. He holds his fingers out of the cage. It is the eternal gesture of hope that says *touch me*.

She knows the rule. Death row inmates are not allowed to have human touch. It is part of their punishment. She could lose her license for that gesture alone. So she gives him another gift instead. She steps just close enough for him to feel her human warmth.

The warden hates her. But how we love her, the lady.

When I first fell so long ago, I was placed in general population—Cellblock A, what they call the Hall of the Lifers.

I knew the dangers of prison for someone like me. I was so scared that I hid in my cell when the doors clanged open for yard times. I waited silently until the other men had all gone down the line, then I slipped along the walls until I made it to the prison library.

I can still remember the path from that cell to the library: two turns with the hand you write. Down the stairs. Then turn the opposite direction, like the way you turn off water.

I wasn't very good at reading back then. The last time I remember being in a real school was when I was eight. It was a little schoolhouse near my grandparents' place. I remember the smell of wet woolen socks on the ancient radiator, and the freshly shaved red neck of the older boy who sat in front of me. Those are the only details I can remember. As for most men in prison, my memories of the outside have become faint over time. The outside world has become the unreal world. When I dream, my dreams are of the inside.

Reading was hard. Even the simple words stumped me. But I kept going back, mostly because I had no other place to go. Eventually, I came to like puzzling over the words in the dusty sunlight that came in the barred windows and lay in long slashes across the wooden table.

Bit by bit it got easier, and when it did, the floodgates opened, and all of a sudden I was reading. I read Nancy Drew and the Hardy Boys. I read Louis L'Amour and the *Encyclopaedia Britannica*, *Wuthering Heights* and the Best American Short Stories collections. I read every book I could on nature, so when the author took us on a walk in the woods, I was there, too. I fell completely for the dark strangeness of Sidney Sheldon and the magic of Ray Bradbury. I read my favorite books over and over again and each time found new things inside them, as if the writers had put in new words in my absence. I'd be reading a passage from my favorite, *The White Dawn*, by James Houston, and all of a sudden there would be a new paragraph that I could swear I had never read before.

I read everything in that dusty little library. I read the prologues and the epilogues until I could tell you how many times Stephen King thanked his wife, Tabitha. I could tell you how the Columbia Indians made their longhouses, or how to make a solar toilet, or how to dry bear meat in the sun. I could tell you all of this if I could talk, but instead the words stayed inside of me and marveled. This I could accept, or so I told myself for a long time. Because the words were there, and they carried me to another place.

After many years of this, the warden came in. The chair I sat in had two deep grooves in the seat where my skinny shanks fit. The area of my table had come to be known as for me and me alone.

The warden was brand-new back then, and a lot younger. His hair was glossy and black, and his face was tanned. He looked like a man who went boating. He held his hand as if proud of his thick gold wedding ring. Everyone joked about how he paraded around his young wife when she visited.

He stood next to my spot at the table where I stacked the books like walls around me. He picked up *Butterfly Collecting for Young Boys*. "Here you are, just like they said," he said.

I nodded, swallowing.

"They say you don't go to the yard or to mess."

No. I shook my head. I wanted to say: The books are enough.

He paused, turning the book over to see a photo of a boy on the back cover. The boy was wearing a short-sleeve shirt. He had a face full of obligatory freckles and a wide innocent smile. He was holding a butterfly net and stood against a field covered in dazzling blue flowers.

"I appreciate you staying out of trouble."

I knew what the warden meant: He appreciated me staying out of the yard, away from the inmates who liked to hurt me, because he was afraid I might someday hurt them back.

"Fellow like you is smart to play it safe," he added, putting the book gently down in front of me.

The other inmates in the library that day were watching all of this with their jaws open. One was a man I knew—he lived in my cellblock. He was a huge, muscled ruddy man with narrow teeth turned in like a rabbit's. I knew as soon as I left, he would lumber up and saunter after me, following me down the dark, empty stairs.

The ruddy man watched the warden talk to me.

His smug grin turned to puzzlement at what the warden did next.

The warden smiled and patted me on the back. The warden—patting me.

And for the next long years of my life, I tried to remember only the reading, not the terrible things that happened to me as I came and went up and down the stairs. The library became my sanctuary. I loved the ways the precious stories took shape but always had room to be read again. I became fascinated with how writers did that. How did they make a story feel so complete and yet so open-ended? It was like painting a picture that changed each time you looked at it.

Some of the things in the books troubled me. The high school biology textbooks reorganized my mind into epicenters of new worlds until the cells of my own walls began to race. The color plates in the medical textbooks showing the insides of people made me shake. It was as if someone had planted these books in the library to remind me of a question that had troubled me for so long: What lives inside the coils inside people? Why did God create us with so many winding, dark puzzles? In times like these, I would have to go back to something comforting like *The White Dawn*.

Sometimes, when reading a book, I would think

of the other people who might have touched it before it was donated. A nice woman who lay down with her baby for a nap might have held the book I was reading. I could see her, lying in a sundress on faded rose-printed cotton sheets, the book splashed open in the sunlight. A little of that sun could have soaked into the pages I was touching.

After a time, it seemed that the world inside the books became my world. So when I thought of my childhood, it was dandelion wine and ice cream on a summer porch, like Ray Bradbury, and catching catfish with Huck Finn. My own memories receded and the book memories became the real memories, far more than the outside, far more even than in here.

But after many more years, I did the other bad thing, and they sent me here.

When you do a really bad thing inside a prison, they don't have many choices. They can kill you and call it an accident, or they can send you into the dungeon. I got sent to the dungeon.

The doors here no longer bang open. If they ever did, I would panic. I would hide on my cot with the blanket over my head. There is no library down the hall with two rights and a left. There is now only me, in my cell, trapped forever. But the trusty still brings me books on his cart.

And the warden comes. Every few weeks he passes my cell, silently pushing a book through the slot. I wait on my cot, blanket over my head, and after I hear the book drop, I scramble for it.

The warden always seems to know which book to bring. When the sun grows dusty hot outside the walls and the sky is gunslinger blue, the warden brings a western. When rain slates against the towers and the world has gone hopeless with gray, it is Bible stories. When the halls ring with the cries of riot and the bars of my own cell rattle with pain, the warden drops a soft book on the floor, solace in its pages: the collected poems of Walt Whitman.

And oh, my favorites, like the tastes of childhood. Every few months the warden passes me *The White Dawn*, and for a few precious days I traverse the open heavens on hard-packed moonlit snow and see the blue splashing arctic lights, and I fill my belly with frozen seal meat and laugh with my Inuit friends.

When I first started reading, I didn't know how to sound some words. I would whisper them inside my head. Sioux, paisley, ruche. Obsolete, rubric, crux. How do you say those words? How do they sound when others say them? Are they as pretty as they sound inside my head?

Once, early on, I tried endlessly to say the word

"Sioux" inside my head. I am still not sure how it sounds. Is the X silent? I would think for hours how strange it was that some parts of words are silent, just like some parts of our lives. Did the people who wrote the dictionaries decide to mirror language to our lives, or did it just happen that way?

I decided that in the end, it doesn't matter. In my mind, the words sound right. They chase each other around like boats on a lake after dusk, and who cares if my metaphors or semicolons or whatever are correct.

The books brought brilliance to my life, and they brought an understanding: Life is a story. Everything that has happened and will happen to me is all part of the story of this enchanted place—all the dreams and visions and understandings that come to me in my dungeon cell. The books helped me see that truth is not in the touch of the stone but in what the stone tells you.

And the stones tell me so much. But if I get some things wrong, then please forgive me. This place is too enchanted to let the story go untold.

The lady stays up late in her apartment, reading York's files.

Death penalty trials come and go like lightning storms, little bursts of electricity in the sky that fizzle and pop, leaving only the smell of ozone and wet newspapers. As soon as the verdict is read, the court staff rolls up boxes and the jurors go home. It is over and forgotten.

Twelve years after his trial, York had run through most of his appeals. He was on the conveyor belt to death. No one noticed, and no one cared. The lady has seen some cases drag on ten, twenty, or even thirty years before the prisoner was executed. Despite the delays, the prison still executes several men every year—there are dozens on the row and more coming all the time. A regular industry, she knows, that pays the keep on both sides.

The lady winces when she reads who were York's trial defense attorneys: two dump trucks widely known as Grim and Reaper for their ability to get their clients killed. They were famous for doing as little as possible while billing as much as possible. But once a man is sentenced to death, she knows, getting death off the table can seem insurmountable, no matter how incompetent the original trial attorneys. A new attorney has to show outrageous violations of the law, or important new evidence that should have been uncovered and presented at trial. As they like to say on the row, York was blood pudding.

So York did the unimaginable thing. He gave up. He renounced his appeals. He said he wanted to die.

All of a sudden the Advocates rose up and the anti-death penalty groups rallied and the money poured in and famous people came begging York to change his mind. He went from another forgotten killer on his way to the chamber to a victim deserving of mercy. The Advocates raised the money to hire decent defense attorneys, and the attorneys hired the best mitigation specialist in the state, all to save the life of a man who had decided to die.

Which is where she comes in.

There are dozens of men on the row who would kill—and she thinks literally—to get her services.

Instead, the honor goes to the one who wants to die. She rubs her tired eyes. They look pink in the light.

She goes to bed in silk pajamas that no one sees. She draws a clean sheet against her scrubbed chin. Her apartment feels empty and cold even to her.

The lady thinks about what it will be like to work this case. She has been a death penalty investigator for eight years. She takes on only one or two cases at a time, hired by attorneys who represent the men on appeal. With more than forty men on the row, that means only a fraction get her services. Usually, she has at least a year to investigate a case. Death penalty investigation is labor-intensive—it takes months to locate ancient records, to track down witnesses from decades before, to plumb the truth of a crime.

Since York denounced his appeals, his execution date has been set—for August 6. The height of summer. She glances at the calendar above her desk. It is May. She has three months to save his life. One season, she thinks, to end an execution.

All of her clients have wanted to live. Some wanted it desperately, others dispassionately. But all wanted it. When she struggles with what she does, she can at least tell herself that she is fulfilling their rights and desires.

Not the case with York.

She thinks about what it will be like to go against a condemned man's wishes, to save him from himself. How does a person know when he wants to die? Is it a flash of light or a slow understanding? Maybe this is just his clever plan to avoid death.

Before she goes to sleep, she thinks, almost unwillingly, about the fallen priest. She sees him striding up to the window, a figure in miniature. His gait is firm and sure. He is wearing the black priest robes he once wore, but he flings them open as if discarding them. When he steps through the glass, she knows she is sleeping, and she dreams all of a sudden that he is there beside her, a little figure that she caresses with care, fearful of breaking.

The guards at the end of the hall are talking about the man they call Arden.

"I hear he's finally coming up," says one.

A hush falls whenever someone brings up the inmate they call Arden. If a prison can have a monster, Arden is ours. In a place full of the worst kinds of killers, his acts alone defy words or explanations. Others may talk about what York did, but no one talks about what Arden did, because some things are too awful to contemplate.

I slide along the rock wall and put my face to the stone and listen.

"It's about time," the other guard says.

"Yeah. Warden says it was one of those things."

I wonder if they mean the man they call Arden is up for parole, but there is no way anyone is granting a monster parole.

"What about York?" The voice is teasing now. The idea of killing York lightens the conversation.

"Are you volunteering for the black shirt?"

There is no answer. They all know the rules—if you volunteer for the execution squad, you don't tell anyone.

"I don't know. Might have a hard time actually killing the asshole, you know."

There is a faintly surprised silence. "Me, too."

The little men with hammers chatter and then shush as well.

Late spring is rampaging outside. Even down in the dungeon, I can tell. The guards bring rain in their hair and on their regulation jackets. They shake it off when they come down the dungeon stairs. A little trickles into my cell. I get down and taste it. It is not the taste of fall rain, which tastes like rotting leaves. It is not the taste of winter rain, which tastes like cold melted ice. No, this is the taste of spring rain, fresh with cut grass and new life.

"Might flood tonight," the guard says outside my cell.

"Shit," the other replies.

I retreat from my bars, wondering why people who live outside choose such ugly words. Maybe that is what happens when you are outside, and the world clangs and barrels and shouts twenty-four hours a day, from your radio your television your wife your neighbor the lawn mower down the street and the scream of airplanes from the sky. Maybe then you use ugly words to tell life to shut up.

The outside is too big and scary for me to think about anymore. The outside is one wild circus where people and ideas clash. I have been inside one locked room or another since I was nine. I am accustomed to it, buried inside rooms that are buried inside other rooms that are buried inside electric razor fences. The walls that might make others feel like they are suffocating have become my lungs.

I sit on my narrow bunk and caress my long yellow toenails and stare at my walls. I think about the river that runs next to our prison, and the pond and how ducks paddle in it. I think about the cold, mucky water and can feel it against my feet, feel the darkness and pull of the swaying weeds below. I pretend my feet are the duck feet, paddling in the sloughs. I taste the muck in my billed mouth, feel the tendons of my feather wings as they pound the slate sky.

Every few years the river rages until it overruns its clay banks, and the muddy slick water races over the parking lot and into the lower levels of our prison, into the basements and especially into our dungeon. Many times over the years I have seen the water slowly bead and then run down my walls and across the floor. Most times it rises only as high as an inch or two, a current that flows mysteriously and delightfully to what I think is the south.

A few times over many, many years, I have seen the water rise as high as my cot. That is when the screaming really starts. The other men are frightened of drowning. I am too busy putting one finger after another in the cold water and feeling the joyous rush to care.

I am too excited to sleep.

Later that night the red warning lights in the hallways flash, trembling with the unseen storm outside. The guards trot down the halls, dragging ancient pumping machines. The machines roar to life with vast gurgling sounds. The underground river is breaching our buried walls; it is seeping and running down into our cave, and I watch it run down my walls. I think about it running in waves down to the caverns below, where the golden horses stomp with delight.

The inmates begin screaming. "What the hell's going on?" They have the panicked voices of men trapped underground. This place is one big grave. But didn't they already know that?

"I ain't Noah, and this ain't the ark!" Striker shrieks from the other cell next to mine.

I am in ecstasy. I place my bare feet against the stone floor and tremble, feeling the first cold trickle, wanting that chilly new information, excited about what chain of life it will tell me about next.

There is a saying among death penalty investigators, the lady knows, that you always end up in the worst house on the block. No matter how poor the neighborhood, no matter how depressing the trailer court, the worst home on the street is always where the family of your client lives. Or the family of the victim.

A colleague of hers used to joke that he didn't even need to pick up cases anymore. He just went to trailer parks and hung out in the worst trailer until he got a new case. Other investigators acted offended, but she understood. That colleague died not long after, out in the field. He knocked on the wrong door, and a man with a sawed-off shotgun blew him away.

She thinks of that investigator as she winds her way through gorgeous blue conifer forests, past glistening rivers and curves that give glimpses of heaven. She is hours out of the city and in a part of the country she never knew existed. This beautiful country, her old friend would say, is not what you expect in death penalty investigations.

She passes elk crossings and small towns with odd old-fashioned names, like Burnt Tree and Hope Creek. The towns are no more than a single store hanging off the side of the road and cabins barely visible in the rising hills beyond. She sees a deer munching grass, unconcerned at the side of the road, her sandy rump showing, her fawn at her side.

As she turns a tree-studded curve, the view opens up to a series of emerald lakes strung out below, like a chain of jewels. The view is jaw-dropping. She sees a small lookout and stops. When she leaves her car, the air tastes impossibly clean.

The glittering lake below is so beautiful, it looks surreal. A red-tailed hawk wheels overhead, and a small bronze plaque tells that the local Native Americans once considered these lakes sacred. Everything was sacred when nothing was taken for granted, she thinks ruefully. She savors the blue forests and endless sky.

When she gets back in her car, she feels mildly depressed. The car smells like stale coffee and soggy sandwiches.

I should move out here, she thinks suddenly. I should rent a little cabin in the woods near these lakes. I could paint or write and clean cabins for a living. Something simple. Or I could just come here. To be away.

The idea grows as she passes more little towns without names and long stretches of nothing but those dappled blue forests, the trees rising over the road and sights of velvet green mossy ground in the forests. She puts down her windows and hears the distant roar of rivers. She imagines what it would be like to live out here, to walk out on the cabin porch every morning with a cup of coffee and see those stellar lakes, to taste the air and fill her eyes with the blue forests. She imagines curling in a white bed under the steep eaves and cooking simple suppers over a one-burner stove. She imagines serving dinner to herself and a man. He sits at the table, a fuzzy silhouette. Her mind turns skittishly away from seeing his face.

The fantasy ends when she turns in to the little town of Sawmill Falls. She drives past a long-closed mill with a caved-in roof alongside a noisy creek and down a street with Closed signs on all the shops. The town appears deserted. She climbs a dirt road that bounces her old car over the ruts. At the top of the dirt road, she finds a smaller road, almost too small to climb, and this takes her to the top of the hill. There she finds a falling-down gate covered with poison oak.

She parks and walks the rest of the way up the road.

Sure enough, the abandoned-looking shack at the top of the hill is the worst home she has seen all day.

"Like I said, I ain't moving much lately."

York's aunt wheezes from her chair. Little tufts of gray stuffing poke through the chair springs. Aunt Beth is a prematurely old woman with wild iron hair and a broad broken smile. She could be forty or she could be seventy. As with most of the poor people the lady meets, poverty has made her ageless. Her swollen feet are in a bedpan full of sudsy-looking water.

"That's Epsom salts, for my feets," she explains.

"My grammy used to do the same thing," the lady says easily, and then thinks, Is that true? Did Grammy soak her feet in Epsom salts? She has no idea, but it doesn't matter. It felt true for the moment.

"So you want me to talk about my nephew," York's elderly aunt says sadly.

"Only if you want," the lady replies gently. She's already explained her job in the simplest form: She is here to learn about York, so the attorneys who represent him can try to save his life.

It takes the old woman a while to warm up, but when she does, all the lady needs to do is listen.

"I remember when my sister had him. He was

a pretty baby. So pretty. But sick, you know? You heard of Shirley, I bet. She never went to England, I'll tell you that. She told stories. But that baby was conceived right here in Sawmill Falls."

"His father?" the lady asks carefully.

"Who knows? She slept with the whole town."

The old woman checks from under shaggy gray eyebrows to see how the lady responds to that information. The lady doesn't respond. In her heart, she just hears warm voices.

"The town must have been bigger back then," the lady finally says, smiling.

The old lady cackles with laughter. "You something."

"What was he like as a little boy?" the lady asks.

"He was—funny. He used to say his bones were on fire. He got sick a lot. Then all of a sudden he changed." She paused. "He stopped saying he was sick. He just got—oh well—different. Shirley didn't know how to raise a child. You know that, right? A horse kicked my sister in the head when she was little, and then she got the vee-dees. You know, the one that goes to your brain?"

"Syphilis," says the lady. She thinks: York's mom had tertiary syphilis of the brain.

"Yes, that's the one. I always felt sorry for Shirley, myself. When she was little, she would open her legs for a piece of candy." The old lady coughs. "The men of this town didn't treat her right." She looks out the broken window, where a scrap of curtain dances in a faint breeze. "Not right at all.

"I tried to take him when he was born, you know. Biggest mistake of my life was giving him back to his mom, even if she was my sister." The old lady rubs one cheek, bringing a spot of rosy color. "Funny how it all comes back. He was sweet as a baby, you know? Sweet as sugar. And then he hardened. I can't 'splain it another way. He was like sugar in a jar that hardens. And after a while you take it out, and it is one rock-solid lump."

The old lady stretches her legs. "Oh, this water feels good. Be a dear and put the pot back on the stove for me? I need a heat-up."

The lady gets up and puts the kettle back on the greasy stove. A coffee can of bacon grease stands on the buckled linoleum counter near the stove. It has fork marks in it. A dirty fork is sitting on the dirty stove near the grease can. The lady looks around the kitchen corner and sees no food.

"By the time he was ten, he was a mean child," the aunt says behind her. "You could tell he wasn't going to be any good."

"Like how?" the lady asks, reminding herself to get some groceries for the aunt before she leaves town.

"I took him in when he was ten. His mama had disappeared again. That was the way with Shirley— she'd take a ride somewhere, and weeks later someone would find her in a ditch someplace. Or she would be down at the mental hospital for her vee-dees. Little York would be alone and nobody would know it. This time I found him in that house, just sitting in the corner like always. He'd been eating the wallboard, he was so hungry." The old woman looks to the lady to see how she takes this news. The lady smiles gently; she has heard far worse, experienced far worse.

"He still didn't want to leave, saying he was waiting for his mama, so I said, 'York, honey, I'll get you a pet if you come with me.' That's how I got him up here. He said, 'Auntie Beth, I want a pet rabbit. A pet rabbit I'm gonna name Troy.' Isn't that funny? Troy. Oh my. So the next day I drove all the way into Burnt County—I could drive back then—and bought him the cutest little white rabbit. Just a doll with pink ears. You could see the veins in those long pink ears."

The lady sits peacefully, listening to the old woman talk.

"He named it Troy, too. That's what got me later— that he named it first. 'Cause as soon as he got that rabbit, he took it from me and said, 'Auntie Beth, I'll be back.' I asked him, 'Where you goin', honey?' And he just smiled and said, 'To the woods.' He came back about an hour later, blood all over his whole body, up his arms and smeared all over his little hands, and that little rabbit pelt dangling from his hand. It looked like a bloody fur jacket for a doll."

The old woman breathes. "You know what he told me?"

"What?" the lady asks.

"He said, 'Troy had a party.'"

The lady leaves much later and buys groceries. She buys a big bag of russet potatoes and beans and bacon and eggs and coffee and a box of powdered milk. Remembering back to her own childhood, she makes sure to get the essentials: shortening and white flour and salt and pepper and a bottle of Tabasco. She throws in a big block of old-fashioned white soap and another bar of Fels-Naptha. For a treat, she picks up the only dusty can of peaches in the town store.

The old woman is ecstatic to get the peaches and insists the lady open them right then and there and pour them into two plastic bowls. The old woman lumbers to her dime-sized porch, and they sit knee-to-knee and eat their peaches.

The sun sets over the scrubby woods below, and the sweet peach juice runs down the lady's throat. It tastes like a miracle.

"No one ever comes to see me," York's aunt says shyly. "Can you come again?"

"I can come again," the lady says, and watches the old woman rock with pleasure as she eats her peaches.

The lady goes down to view the chamber where York wants to die. She doesn't need a pass or permission. It is no secret. They even bring walking tours down.

The Chamber of the Vine is at the far end of our dungeon, down a narrow hallway where the walls continually weep moisture and strange toadstools grow in the corners. When men walk this hall, they know it is their last journey. Only those who work here return the way they came.

The priest's office is near the Chamber of the Vine, so he can give prayers to the condemned men. The prison goes through a priest every few years. Usually, the priests make it through a handful of executions and then leave. Most are still wet behind the ears and using the job as a stepping-stone for better positions. It sounds important to be a death row priest. But few can last long in the casual atmosphere of death. The warden is betting the fallen priest is so shamed by being fallen that he might be hopeless enough to last—an angel with clipped wings in our midst.

The lady walks past the office of the priest. She looks in his window, hoping to see him, but his desk is empty. His office is cluttered and yet seems lonely. There is a plant with dust on the leaves, dying for lack of sunlight. There are books everywhere, falling over the shelves and piled on his desk. An empty coffee cup waits.

The door to the death chamber is open.

The Chamber of the Vine is small and painted bright orange. Perhaps the orange color was meant to look cheerful. Instead, it looks nauseating. The paint has peeled off the eternally damp stones, falling in long orange pieces to the floor. The pieces are swept up before each execution.

There is a large window made of heavy safety glass set in the far wall. Through it, the lady can see the small room where they allow the witnesses. Folding chairs are stacked against the wall.

A greasy old black phone hangs from the wall. A peeling grimy white sticker on it says SUPREME COURT.

The lady sniffs. There is no smell of death, though men die here all the time. There is only a smell of disinfectant that can barely hide the wet mildew smell of river.

She touches the table in the middle of the room. It is as narrow as a graveyard slab, covered with a thin sheath of black vinyl. The vinyl is so when the men soil themselves, as they often do in the posture of death, the table can be wiped clean easily. Straps hang from the sides. The canvas straps are old and frayed but as strong as steel. The buckles are metal and rusted.

At least a hundred men have died here, she thinks, and feels inside herself for a response. She is not sure she has one.

The lethal injection machine is standing near the table. It looks a bit like a fuse box with an open door. Instead of fuses, there are milky tubes topped with injector buttons. The tubes feed in to the IV bag, which snakes cloudy tubes onto the floor.

At the base of the machine is a set of control buttons. The red buttons are labeled: ARMED, START, and finally, FINISH.

"See something?" It is a voice behind her.

She turns, her bones turned liquid with shock. She hates being surprised. It is the priest, as warm and cautious as ever. He is wearing the same oxford shirt as always, the same trousers hanging on his thin frame. His eyes look haunted. She wonders if he knows how much pain is visible in his eyes.

She touches the machine and hesitates. "Do you ever think they deserve to die?" she finally asks.

"I'm a Catholic priest," he says with a startled laugh. "Or I was."

"We all die," she says. "For some it just comes earlier."

He steps closer so he can look into her face. Concern has etched his brow. "Life has meaning," he says.

She feels more naked than ever before. She thinks of York and his mother. She thinks of his pet rabbit. Her eyes feel suddenly wet. "There is too much pain in the world, that's the problem," she says, her voice low and husky.

"Pain and beauty, and beauty in the pain." His voice is a whisper that strokes her.

She looks up at him. His eyes meet hers. For the first time she feels a connection with him. It feels like a warm current. It feels like electricity. It feels like warmth that has been born in her belly.

Back so long ago, when they built this enchanted place, they killed men in three ways: They waited for them to die, they worked them to death, and they hanged them.

Not much has changed. Instead of working men to death, there is a slow starvation of the body and soul. And instead of rope, they use a machine.

I once overheard a guard say that in the beginning, they hanged because rope was cheap. Then they stopped and went to guns—firing squads. Bullets got expensive, and blood is messy. Brains and blood, who wants to clean that up? Then came the electric chair, but that wasn't what it promised to be, either: too many dancing corpses. After an execution, the guard joked, the place reeked like a bad hair salon. Finally, they sent the scientists to invent the easiest and cleanest way to die. They came up with the Chamber of the Vine.

I used to wonder, Who invented this miracle machine? Then one day in the library, I read the man's name. It was one of the few times I have felt disappointed by reading. A name has no meaning, you see, unless you see the bodies attached, like a man paddling down a river, dragging a sea of corpses.

I think that in the outside world, names come with meanings. A Harriet might bring forth a Samuel, and he is followed by a Dan, maybe, or a Susan. The names are connected like cords of life, each breathing into another, and those names go searching to breathe into others, so the whole idea of a family tree is not a dead spine but a living, breathing thing, with roots under clean soil, and bright sparkling branches hungry for the sky. When someone dies in the outside world, the other names go on breathing, seeking, creating, so that the tree seeds into the fertile forest floor, and it all continues.

In here, names end. We end. Like periods end sentences. Like the ropes and the bullets and the hot electric nodes and the frying chair and, eventually, the cool milky tubes. Even if we live out our lives in here, we end. Our creation is over.

No one knows this more than the corpse valets.

Late at night we hear the metal clacking of the wheels—creakety-clack, creakety-clack!—and ev-

ery man in here knows what it means: The corpse
valets are coming.

Inside their cells, the men listen, even in their
sleep, so that the sound of the wheels entwines with
their dreams—so that years after a release, a man
might stop short at the sound of a metal cart passing, not knowing why he is flooded with sadness
and fear.

Only the dead know the corpse valets—the dead
and the guard called Conroy, who decides which inmates can be selected for this duty. It has to be a man
who knows how to be quiet; how to keep secrets.

And the secrets are so many. How bodies end up
dead in cells with signs of strangulation or broken
necks, and the guards clear their throats and say
natural causes. How others are shot and others die
in heaps of blood all erased by the dawn. How no
one ever dies here of abuse, of rape, of being killed
by the guards. How the records—what records? A
prison is a place without history.

Almost every night, the corpse valets collect the
dead. Even down here in the dungeon, I hear them,
pushing their squeaking carts down the stone halls
far above me. They come here, too, after every execution. The door slams, and the men down the row
turn their faces to the walls, afraid to see the care-
takers of death pushing their cart. Really, there is

nothing to see. Even under their hoods, their faces are folded into themselves. If you were to touch them, they would disappear, like smoke.

The corpse valets are one of the secrets of this place. Like the endless basements that coil like giant serpents, waiting to open their oven mouths. Like the jaws of the flibber-gibbets. Like the names in the books of the dead that lift from their pages at night to float into the sky, turning the stars into letters that anyone can read.

I think what it would be like to be a corpse valet. To lift bodies and feel the weight of their passing. How odd it is, that the dead weigh more than the living. You would think it would be the opposite, but it isn't. I think it is because souls give bodies lightness and air. When the soul leaves, the body has nothing left and is desperate to return to the earth. That's why it's so heavy.

Others might feel sorry for the corpse valets. They say that once you're a corpse valet and know so many terrible secrets, the prison cannot let you go.

I like to listen for the sounds of their creaking wheels late at night. I like to think about their passage across the dusty yards in the earliest of morning, when the mist rises off the river and the geese come swooping in, crying at the wonder of life. What a beautiful thing that must be, to feel the weight of the dead even as the earth rises and is born again.

York is furious that the lady has seen his aunt.

He glares at her from the wooden bars of the Dugdemona cage, his eyes like obsidian. His hands grip the bars. She can see the tensed anger in his body, the barely contained rage that lives inside so many of her clients. She is suddenly glad for the chains, glad for the cage, glad for the keepers at the door.

"You didn't have my permission to talk to her," York hisses.

Usually, she cultivates these death row clients for months. She builds a castle for them in the Dugdemona cage where they reign as kings. They feel safe in that castle, so they can tell her their terrible, shameful secrets. From her own history, she knows how strong that castle has to be, how deep its moat of protection has to be to let a grown child tell the world buried secrets. At each and every step, she asks their permission. "Is it okay if I talk to your mom?" or "Do you mind if I visit your aunt?" She knows condemned men feel powerless. In the secret castle they build together in the Dugdemona cage, she gives them power.

But York is already scheduled for execution. She doesn't have time to bring him along. Besides, he told her he wants to die. So she ignored this critical permission-gathering step. She realizes now that was a tactical mistake. She tells herself she needs his cooperation to do her job, if nothing else.

"I'm sorry I went behind your back," she says.

"What did my aunt say?" His voice is naked.

"She said she still loves you, despite what you did."

His hands drop from the cage bars. The dark eyes soften. "Auntie Beth."

"She told me about the rabbit."

He just looks at her. Now he is on firmer ground. Killing things is his specialty.

"Who was Troy?" she asks.

The hawk eyes get bewildered, and he pushes off the bars, and with a flash, she sees it, buried deep in his soul.

A familiar, small, sad bell of recognition rings inside her. It is only here, with men in the Dugdemona cage, that she gets to hear the bittersweet sound of that bell, ringing from her past into the present. She knows now what she needs to do.

The next visit with Auntie Beth comes on a Saturday.

The lady likes to travel on Saturdays. The roads are mostly clear, and the world feels like a weekend. Probably because it is, she teases herself.

The drive is even better than before. She thinks she could drink the blue-forested beauty forever, and when she gets to the chain of lakes, she holds her breath. She stops at the same lookout to see the glittering, gorgeous waters, the tall trees around her. She hears the small sounds of a forest alive: birds, the rush of wind in the tall branches, the sound of water chapping at the shore.

Now she understands what people mean when they say they fell in love with a place. She isn't sure it is love, but it is peace. She breathes deep and lets the blue air cleanse her soul. She stops at a little bakery along the way, then a decent grocery store.

Auntie Beth is overjoyed to see her. She sees the lady has brought another bag of groceries—*You shouldn't have!*—and a small brown paper bag dotted with grease stains and emitting the most heavenly aroma of fresh donuts.

Auntie Beth ducks her head as she eats the donuts, wiping the crumbs from her mouth. The two talk about a lot of things. They talk about baking; the old woman used to make all her own bread. They talk about kids. Beth says she never had any of her own. She was a spinster. "Maybe my sister turned me off of all that," she says. They talk about shame and life and the deep orange color of a good farm egg.

The lady tells Auntie Beth a little about herself. It is odd how comfortable she is, telling these people—the families of her clients—details about her life that she would never tell her colleagues. But she knows Aunt Beth will understand. And she knows that with the channel opened between them, Aunt Beth will share.

When Auntie Beth is ready, they talk about York's mother.

"Shirley was the sweetest little sister," Auntie Beth says. "I was older, you know, but not by much. Those were the days! The log trucks burned up the roads back then, and one tree could fill a truck. Nowadays you got all the spotted owls and the tree huggers. I grant you, they were right, because there ain't no woods left around here anymore. Just scrub and poison oak like you see now. But back then, the town was full."

She ruminates for a while, looking at the distant clouds from her porch. "It was the horse kick. They didn't know what to do back then. No extra rays or nothing. Just put some dressing on it. Like the vee-dees she got later. The town doctor didn't do nothing for that," Auntie Beth spits with some venom. "By the time she had my nephew, every man in the town had her. Things happened I won't name. It was like the whole town, all the menfolk, went crazy on that girl. And the women just watched and smirked and let it happen. Even my own family."

The lady watches as a tear floats down Auntie Beth's wrinkled face. "You know why?" the old lady asks.

The lady shakes her head.

"She was beautiful, that's why. I got a picture."

Auntie Beth lumbers to her swollen boat feet and makes her painful way into the main room, where she opens a rickety wooden drawer and takes out an ancient photograph. She offers the photo as if it is worth more than a bar of gold.

The lady accepts it with the same reverence. It is a black-and-white photograph of a beautiful young woman with pale skin, wide eyes, and silky dark brown hair. There is something disconcerting about the blankness in her eyes. It is strange and yet an invitation. Take me, her eyes say. I am as blank and deep as the emerald lakes outside your door.

Sitting on the woman's lap is a little boy. It is York, the lady realizes, looking too young and innocent to ever be a killer. The only known photograph of him as a child has been hiding here in his aunt's shack for twenty years. Before, he was a demon without a past. Now he was once a child.

The lady can see now what Beth meant—how York was as sweet as sugar before he hardened. He had a hopeful, tremulous smile. Perhaps the photographer was promising candy when they were done.

"Just a baby back then," Auntie Beth says, and reaches for the photograph. "Funny teeth."

The lady broaches the subject carefully. "Maybe sometime, if you are okay with it, I can borrow that and make a copy."

"Why, sure, I trust you," Auntie Beth says, and goes to get a used envelope to tuck the precious photograph inside. "Anyone who knows her donuts gets my love." And they both laugh.

She leaves Auntie Beth's home early enough to get back in the town of Sawmill Falls before the dinner hour. She feels a little sick from all the donuts and the coffee Auntie Beth made, which was thin but bitter enough to cut rope. Only after she drank it did the old woman tell her, with some mischief in her eyes, that she reused the coffee grinds for weeks to save money. "I steeps them in hot water," she said.

The town of Sawmill Falls is dusty and dead. There is the solitary store, which she already knows has one mysterious aisle devoted to boxes of dream mix coated with dust, years past any expiration date—if such stuff expires. She wanders a bit with the roar of the creek in the background. There is only one street, so there is not far to wander.

After the economy collapsed following the mill closure, the townspeople apparently tried to find other ways to make money. The two-block main street has boarded-up signs for the Bead Store Emporium and Nature's Gifts. She has come to recognize bead stores as indicators of economic doom. She peeks in the soaped window and sees empty shelves and the velvet antlers of a cheap necklace tree on the floor.

Farther down the street, she finds a single small brick building with boarded windows. A creaking sign outside has a board swinging. It advertises that the building was once the town law firm, post office, and doctor's office.

It *was* a bigger town then. The lady imagines how the loggers would come in from the hills after working for weeks in the company longhouses in the woods, to spree on liquor, and the country folk coming in from afar looking for their mail, shy and uncertain in the big town. She could imagine the moms lining up at the post office to mail their holiday letters and the children hopping foot to foot, excited to see if the eagerly awaited Sears catalog had arrived, to be thumbed for months before Christmas. She could picture the young couples coming to town with their new babies, taking them to the doctor to be weighed and measured and inoculated.

And she could envision Shirley, traipsing the dusty street in a dirty dress, as fond as a flower, her vacant eyes turned happily to any face. The lady could imagine how the town women hated her. They saw her as different, thinking she chose to be the way she was. They didn't see the damage behind the beautiful face.

The lady realizes she has stopped. She doesn't know why she has stopped and turned around. She is staring at the creaking sign over the closed brick building. It takes her a time, listening to the raging creek off the main road. Sounds come from a distance to her in times like this, when life rages in a vacuum backward.

The dust smell climbs in her nose, and the episode passes without her falling to her knees in a full-fledged déjà vu attack, which is always embarrassing.

It is the sign. For the town doctor: Dr. Hammond.

It is the thought that has been coalescing in the back of her mind for days. York's mother was the town slut, she thinks, the brain-damaged girl who spread her knees for a nickel.

All those men and only one son?

The lady is close to the city when she realizes that hours have passed, and she didn't even see the highways. Night fell long ago. She was in a reverie.

She was remembering sitting under the bushes in her backyard as a child. It was her secret place. The bushes were large, overgrown laurel hedges, and inside she had made a sort of cave. She took things into the cave sometimes—a piece of soft cloth to touch, a dirty plastic toy teakettle to pretend. Mostly, she just took herself.

What did she think about during those endless hours in the laurel hedge? As a child, she made an imaginary world so real that she could feel and taste it today. Sometimes she would imagine that she and her mom lived on a magical island where the trees dripped fruit. Other times they traveled all over the world, just the two of them, like the best of buddies. In all the stories, her mom was whole and she was safe. When she left the laurel hedge, she would bend the thick green leaves back, to hide where she had been. And when she came back the next day, crawling with a sandwich she had made of stale bread with the mold cut off and hardened peanut butter from the jar, the magic world would be waiting for her.

She wonders if York had a magic world, too. A magic world away from the pain and terror of his life. She wonders if he had a safe place he could take himself, a place to shelter the tender nugget of life within, or if he was naked and open all the way, to whatever walked through his mother's door.

When I read a book now, I hold it under the light above my cot. The bulb is dim in its wire cage. But if I sit just right, I can catch a segment of gray light without the wire cage marks. My eyes are getting old. I have to squeeze them sometimes to see the words.

Long ago, in the library, I sat on the table under a cloud. The little dust motes would fly in the window and hang above me like a halo or God in the sunlight.

For a long time I thought maybe those little sparks were creatures. They could be creatures almost too tiny to see, just a little taste on the tip of your tongue. Maybe God sent them, like fire creatures, like the sparks before the beginning of life, or maybe the dust that rises from your hair after you're dead. I would stop reading and crane my neck back to watch them swarm above me. The other inmates would jab each other and point, but I didn't care.

Later I read that there *are* things inside us too tiny to see. Not even a microscope can capture them. This got me thinking—if there are things inside us too tiny to see, might there be things outside us too big to believe?

I was nine when I went into the hospital. The police showed up at the run-down hotel where my mom and I were staying. They took one step inside and saw. I remember one officer covering my naked body with his blue rain jacket before he took me to his car.

They took me to a foster home, but I kept running away—running to find my mom. Finally, the foster parents gave up. No one wanted a boy who didn't talk, a boy who sat in the corner and growled, a boy caught trying to cut open his own belly with a razor.

STATE HOSPITAL FOR THE INSANE said the script above the front door. Back then they had a children's ward. The children's ward was a tall concrete building painted a dismal pink, with rust stains running from the bars like long red tears. In the middle of the night, we would pull our mattresses out into the hallway so the lights from the windows at either end of the hall would illuminate what the guards otherwise would not see.

It was there they said I had selective mutism and

a bunch of other words like *antisocial* and *conduct* and *disorder*. I didn't agree with those words and I still don't. People try to make names for things they don't understand. They want to contain people in jars like dead babies.

I was in that place for almost ten years. I got used to it—used to the sound of soda cans clunking down the machine in the staff room late at night when the custodians came, used to the constant light in the white rooms, used to the restraints and the smell of piss when you couldn't hold it anymore, used to the lost months of Haldol and strange dreams of Thorazine, used to the terror of night, used to the parade of therapists and counselors and doctors who came through with rancid breath that smelled of coffee and anxiety, and sweaty fingers grasping my file, promising they would stay when always they would leave, until they merged into one long watery face.

And then one day I was eighteen and they said, "Okay, time to leave."

It turned out I had been a ward of the state. Once I turned eighteen, no one was paying for my keep. They gave me a folder with my papers and showed me to the front door. I stepped under that carved mantel and walked outside down a long lane lined with trees. It was windy and cold that day. A gardener pointed the way to the city.

The wind came down and stole the papers from my hands, and I opened my palms and let them go.

I stopped at the first home I saw, a little ranch with a clothesline in the back and a window with a fluttering white curtain.

It takes a week for the lady to locate the retired Dr. Hammond of Sawmill Falls. She feels the clock ticking and York smiling as time passes with no progress. Every day that passes with no results, he has told her with his notched smile, is like a dime in the bank for his death.

His execution date is circled in red on her calendar. She picked up the case in May; already it is closing in on June.

Dr. Hammond of Sawmill Falls has retired to a nameless bedroom community on the outskirts of the city where she lives. The homes all look alike, perched in orderly formations on the hillsides, their dying yards spackled with forgotten shrubs.

He is not happy to see her. Fortunately, she doesn't care.

She had worried the doctor was dead, but no, he is older than Aunt Beth and tottering. He totters into the dark living room with an impatient air. He totters to his liquor cabinet. He totters to get a clean glass, which is really spotted. He totters around his house, which is like a dollhouse for saints. He has a nativity scene on the mantel. The objects people put out for viewing in their homes fascinate her.

She has come to believe that the homes of sad or hateful people smell different. When people have sadness or hate inside them, it comes out in a miasma. Dr. Hammond's house smells like a form of slow poison has been hanging in the air for years. She has a sudden conviction that if she lifted all the furniture in his house, she would find layers of squished black bugs underneath.

Right away he says he knows nothing. He remembers nothing. He could guest-star on *Hogan's Heroes* as the bumbling know-nothing Sergeant Schultz.

"I don't know that woman," he says again.

She wonders if getting affidavits from Auntie Beth about her damaged sister and her little son will be enough to convince the judges to spare York's life, especially when they know he wants to die. No. For a case like this, she needs the brass ring—something so irreversibly altering that it cannot be denied for post-conviction relief.

"Nope, never heard of her," he says, and lifts his drink with a shaky hand.

You liar, she thinks. She wants to kick him in his skinny shanks. She wants to tear the nativity scene off the polished mantel and throw it in his lame fake fireplace. Instead, she turns on her empathy high beam. You are a water bug on the surface of life, Dr. Hammond, she thinks, and I am the fish coming to feed.

"It must have been hard to be the town doctor," she says in a soft voice.

"Come again?"

"So many people coming to you with so many problems." She makes her eyes soft. "I bet a lot of them were, you know, woods folk. Not too bright. And you were a *doctor*."

His eyes are uncertain. "I don't remember the lady you talked about."

"Of course not. I think I was wrong about her, wrong name, sorry, no big deal. I obviously got the wrong person." She is stepping back in her tracks oh so carefully. "I know what it's like to be the only qualified person in a place. The only one who understands."

She thinks, What a lie. You barely graduated from high school and slogged through community college having no idea of what you would become, just knowing you had to find it. You fell into this work because you know what it is like to live like Shirley, to live like York, to live like all the others and not like this man.

And yet in the moment, it is always true. It is true because her own childhood taught her how to pretend to be like the others just to survive, all the while protecting her pure, untouched core.

He has met her eyes with his blood-mapped own. "It was hard," he agrees. "I had degrees, you know. I was a *doctor.*"

She smiles and relaxes into her chair. She is going on a journey to the past. She will go with him and see what is there.

It takes hours, but Dr. Hammond finally gives her the information she needs without even knowing it. He tells her that when he retired—you would think Rome had to be notified—he sent his few remaining patients to a doctor in a nearby town. And along with them went all of Dr. Hammond's medical records.

The lady waits her turn at the old metal detector, which the guards joke is there to give her cancer. To judge by the creaking high-pitched hum of the ancient machine, she is not sure they are joking. The windows inside the prison lobby are glossed white with foulness, the fake leather seats ripped and slashed. The fat trusty is there to fix the ailing Coke machine. He gives her a distrustful look, glancing at the lanyard on her chest.

She sees the priest come in, take off his loafers. She smiles at his bare feet. It is a wonder they let him get away with that.

The priest stands in line behind her, painfully aware of her presence. There are three electric inches between them. He glances down to her folding shoulder blades, the smallness of her back, the curve under her skirt. The trusty smirks.

The visiting sergeant signals the lady forward, through the hum of the machine. She carries nothing metal: no jewelry, no watch, no phone, no pens or hair clips. Her hands are empty except for a single piece of paper.

The priest unloads pockets full of random items: paper clips, loose keys, cards with magnetic strips, an old falling-apart wallet. His cheeks grow flushed as he fills the plastic tray, and then he is signaled through. She smiles as he fills his pockets.

They walk down a very steep, long corridor that leads down into the bowels of Cellblock A, where another guard awaits to usher them through the series of locking doors that will take them deeper and deeper into the prison, down below to the final stairwells leading into our dungeon.

The lady is silent as they pass through the thunderbolts of the locks. She holds the lanyard on her chest like a security talisman. The guards look at the priest with contempt. The lady, they eye carefully. The warden has warned them about her; she is not there to do them any good.

The priest walks next to her. He is aware only of her scent—soap and fresh air.

They are almost down to the dungeon when the lady seems to sense him and turns to look up at him. She is down below, and he is here, and what is she to do with this warm body among the almost dead. She cannot stop them all from dying, and so she knows that the noises of their breathing and snoring and pleas behind the bars are all pathetic offerings against the reality of time running out. She cannot begin to care who breathes and who dies down here, because if she did, it would crush her.

The priest seems to understand—he does without speaking. His eyes are on her as if he is trying to pull something out of his chest. As if he is administering not to the dead but to someone who might care.

"I'm not signing that," York says, looking at the medical release in her hand.

The lady gets close to him in the cage. Not close enough so he can reach but within an inch of his possible grip. "I know you say you want to die," she says, and her voice is calm and hard. "I respect your choice."

"Then you don't need that paper," he says with a flick of his dark eyes.

She looks again at the medical release. She meets his eyes. Both are struck again by how similar they look—like dark woods creatures slinking out of fern and clover. They could be brother and sister for how alike they look.

"You know what I am trying to do," she says. "I'm trying to save you from execution. And unlike most of my clients, you don't want to be saved. But I want it."

"Why? Because you *love* me?" His voice is snide. "Because you *care*?"

"No." She feels her voice turn into a calm river.

"Why, then?"

"It's my job."

For the first time, she sees a light in his dark eyes. She can see what a strangely charismatic man he was, despite his oddly formed little body. She can see how easy it was for him to do those terrible things. To real women like her.

He bursts out laughing, those strangely notched teeth thrown back. "So it's not about me," he says. "You're different. I heard that before, but it's true."

She leans over. "I'm going to build you a castle," she says.

"Yeah?" He sounds amused.

The amusement dies when she comes close enough to the cage that he could grab her, but she acts as if she knows he will not, and she is right. He can see the determination in her eyes. "We don't have much time."

He returns her chilly gaze. "I still want to die."

"I know."

The bouncing ball, as she hopes, takes her back out to the blue country. She packs an overnight bag so she can take her time and then find a motel room. Maybe she can even find a cabin along those emerald lakes. The idea fills her with a delicious, unexpected anticipation.

The town is called Squiggle Creek. It isn't much farther past Sawmill Falls, down roads that whip and twist, and the sense of déjà vu grows as she travels, until she becomes convinced she may never find her way home, and she would not argue with it, being lost in these blue woods.

The last doctor has died, but he left his records in the hands of his daughter, who runs a café and bakery in the building where her father practiced. Luckily, the daughter has stored all her father's medical records in the dusty attic. "I keep telling myself to get rid of these things," she says as the lady follows her broad rump up the creaking pull-down attic stairs.

An hour later, with dust on her shirt, the lady carries a thin folder with two names crookedly typed on the outside. In the other hand, she has a white paper bag with a thick turkey sandwich she has bought from the daughter in the coffee shop, who looked at the lady's small frame with pity before adding an extra swipe of cooked salad dressing from what looked like a handmade crock.

The lady stops at the aptly named Squiggle Creek on her way out of town. She crosses a little footbridge and carefully slides down the bank to where the stream narrows into a deep pool. She sits at the edge on a boulder and eats her sandwich. After the first startled bite, she realizes it is made out of chunks of real turkey from some leftover bird, along with a tangy cranberry relish and that fresh old-fashioned cooked dressing, all on two thick doorstops of homemade white bread. The sandwich is satisfying in a way most food isn't to her. She eats the whole thing and watches the baby fish come up to the edge of the bank, nibbling at the pebbles. The fresh tumbling water makes her think of drinking and thirst and the hunger she has always felt—if she could swim in this creek, and wade away to forever, she might be whole.

A man comes down the bank. He is tall and thin, with graying sideburns, and dressed in old jeans and a pair of battered cork boots. He carries a fishing pole in one hand, his other fingers laced into the plastic-ring top of a six-pack.

He gives her a simple, affectionate woods smile. "Afternoon," he says.

"Afternoon. Where does this creek go?" she asks.

"Where they all do, I guess."

She smiles. "Where's that?"

"The lakes."

She rises and dusts the crumbs from her slacks. Her bottom feels cold from the boulder. "Do the people round here ever call them anything but the lakes?"

He looks amused. "No, ma'am. Just the lakes."

"And why is that?" she asks. She says this in a playful voice but suddenly the answer seems very important to her, and this tall woodsman with his gentle smile seems safe to give it.

"Well—I suppose some things don't need names, do they, ma'am?"

She smiles and it is like a sudden lifting of her spirits, a real sunshine smile. "No," she says, still grinning hugely at him, and he is grinning back. "Some things don't need names."

It is dusk by the time she gets back to the lakes, and she has a headache from peering over the steering wheel as she turns the dark forested corners. She is convinced she will not find a place to stay and will be forced to drive in the dark through the woods.

Then she sees a neon Vacancy sign on the side of the road. It is an old-fashioned road motel, with small cabins along the lake's edge.

She parks in the little asphalt lot. She is almost shaking as she gets out of her car. A flood of emotions has come over her. She walks down to the water's edge. The emerald lake spreads in front of her, the caps of water lit with gold tints from the fading sun. Powerful smells come across the waters on a cool breeze: fir and cedar, water and fish, deep growing things and all the weight of the surrounding forests. It is as if the blue forests want to say *breathe* to her, and she wants to say back, *yes*.

She gets the room key from an old woman who doesn't even come up to her chin. The woman has a Greek accent, and on the tiny chipped counter next to the register, she has an array of homemade goodies wrapped loosely in waxed paper. "You take a treat?" she asks, handing the lady a palm-sized pastry along with her key. The whole scene begins to feel surreal, and the lady worries briefly that she is having another déjà vu episode. She knows she is not. She is experiencing something for the first time in her life—a sense of place. This is a good place, her body tells her.

The lakeside cabin is old but clean, with a warm sense that someone actually has been there, wiping the counters and shaking out the homemade quilt.

The minute she sits on the soft bed, she has a strong urge to call the priest. *Come home*, she wants to say, which is strange, because she has never wanted to call him before.

She turns on the old television and dials through a comforting static before realizing there are only three channels out here. She turns off the television. She sits on the edge of the bed eating her pastry, which crackles with honey and walnuts. She hears an owl call and a break of brush from an animal, hears a television in another room and a woman's voice and the sound of water lapping against the shore. She lies down and thinks of the laurel hedge of her childhood, and the magical world inside it, and how she could never tell anyone that even now, as she drifts to sleep, she imagines a place where she can feel whole.

Back in her cold city apartment, the lady reads the old medical records for York and his mother. His attorneys will be happy, she knows, when she tells them.

What the attorneys don't know is the fever that follows finding poison.

Her clients rarely walk to freedom—that is a myth. She can count her truly innocent clients on one finger. Most of the men she works with are guilty. They may not be guilty of all they were charged, but they are guilty of more than enough. Many are guilty of even worse, the crimes that were suspected and never proved.

No, the dream of the death row client is to escape execution for a life behind bars. They want to escape the dungeon into the rest of the prison. They want a visit from their mom that involves a touch. They want to stand in the sun, to play a game of ball, to eat at a table with other men, to see the sky and feel the wind. Those are their dreams, maybe small to others but huge to them. It is a modest dream, in a sense, and yet one that is amazingly hard to achieve for a man on death row.

At least all of her clients have wanted that except for one—York.

The lady goes to bed and thinks of a beautiful girl who managed to have "miscarriage" after miscarriage starting at age eleven, until by some miracle she avoided Dr. Hammond's abortion fish hook until it was too late and she gave birth to a little baby boy when she was sixteen. In a note at the bottom of York's birth record, the doctor had scribbled, *Sterilized.* There was no consent form or signature.

Shirley probably didn't even know that Dr. Hammond had done it—so the town men could go on fucking her without recourse or retribution. She was a little girl who displayed obvious signs of the brain damage and venereal disease that would take her life. Only instead of receiving help, she was passed around like a broken toy.

What was it like? It had to be a dark time for the town. Maybe it played as much a role in the town's decline as the death of timber, as guilty souls and angry women slunk away and a vacant, beaten Shirley was left to wander the streets with a malnourished little boy in her arms.

And as for little York? His medical records were cursory, as if Dr. Hammond didn't have the time to bother with the unwanted. But each limited entry told a terrible story. Dislocated hips at age one—as if someone had spread his little legs into a frog shape and pressed with adult weight. Strange illnesses that came and went. Burns to the arms at age two. A "wet gray fungus" growing near his anus for the better part of a year when he was only three. *Will not respond to sulfur*, the doctor had written, and seemed to give up until the fungus went away on its own. Missing clumps of hair. Partial unexplained deafness. Broken toes, lacerations, burns to fingers.

If child abuse had a record, this was it.

And each time the good Dr. Hammond bandaged the child of the town slut and sent him back to whatever hell he lived in.

She sleeps and she dreams, hot dreams, and several times she startles awake, knowing she has shouted something into the empty night. The nightmares are back. She dreams of glittering knives and of men falling to earth in boxcars from heaven. She dreams of men who lie on children, breaking their little hips into frog shapes. The men pull out knives and flay the toddlers, holding the wet skins like flags in the night. She is in her damp childhood bed again, listening for footsteps in the dark.

A man is standing by her bed. He turns into York. He is holding a knife.

Tit for tat, York says in her dreams while he slashes. *Tit for tat.*

It is always like this. The nightmares are like some loathsome midnight monster that spawns whenever she is deep inside a case, when she begins to see the person who did the terrible things. She becomes his heart, his family, his victim.

She thinks of York's mother, and she turns her face to the wet pillow and dreams again.

Years ago, when I was general population in the cellblock far above me, I had a little window. I was lucky to have that slot of stone, barred with iron, that gave my nose air and, if I wanted to pull up with my aching arms, a view of the sky.

Down below that window was the yard I avoided.

During the days, I could hear the crash of metal, hear the catcalls of my tormentors. I would crouch under that window, convinced they could see through the stone.

But in the evenings? I had the freedom of a view.

The lip of that sill lifted me to my heaven. At dusk, when the yard cleared and no one was around but the walking shadows, I could see into the world itself.

As the night around me fell during those days, I could hear the men down the halls going to mess or the showers or the activities room—the faint din of thousands of men as they buried their ways inside the emptiness of our walls. That was when the yard was cool and serene and empty.

That was when I would perch, remembering the books I had stored in my heart that day to forget the ache and sadness of my body. I would hold myself on that windowsill and just look into the yard below. So beautiful it was, filled with soft shadows. How the dust looked as the sun fell, like freshly driven snow. How the baseball diamond glowed to where I could see the reason for the name. How the guard towers softened in the falling light, and the guards held their night rifles like dark toys.

Bit by bit the sun would go down, and the sky would fade to purple and then to close, and the faintest stars would twinkle beneath the dusk, and the yard seemed truly empty—and waiting. The air glowed before the night canvassed the sky with blackness.

That was when I would see the soft-tufted night birds.

I never knew when the birds would come. It might be one night out of three for weeks or only once an entire year. Like the golden horses or the men with hammers, the birds were free. On lucky nights, they would appear out of nowhere and fall out of the sky like soft darts from heaven. One, two, three. Four and then many.

I could see them so clearly from my cell window—see their soft warm bodies, warm bundles of gray and brown feathers, see the spread of their brown tails and the tilt of their inquisitive heads as they fell past me. Their eyes were warm and dark and all-seeing, like the eyes of the lady.

The first bird would always land in the yard and waddle out to the middle, alone. As if that gray expanse were nothing to her, as if it took no courage. And then following her with mincing steps came the other birds, as if heralding her courage. They would lower their wings and dance around her like a ballet. As much as she preened, you could see she was alone out there, plain and dowdy.

The other birds would spread their soft pum-
meled wings, like graphite mixed with brown stone.
Tiny steps at first, tracing their very wingtips in the
dust, and then greater steps that were not broader or
bigger but were somehow stronger, like the stamp-
ing of tribal feet. The birds raised their claws and
traced those wings through the dust, and after a
while I saw that they left a pattern—a life pattern.

Sometimes I wanted to clap my hands to see
what would happen. Of course I never would do
that. I just watched, holding perfectly still, a lone
face embedded in the stone.

For at least an hour, the soft-tufted night birds
would dance, tracing their circles in the dust until
the entire yard was decorated with the lace of their
efforts.

And then all at once, as if a silent explosion had
happened elsewhere, as if an alarm had sounded in a
distant sky, the soft-tufted birds would stop, freeze,
and look up. One by one the females would lift dun
wings and take flight. Their forlorn male dancers
would rise reluctantly after them until the dark
purple sky was filled with their churning wings.

And then the sky was empty. The brown birds
and their soft-tufted angel boys were gone.

I would watch them go and wonder about where
they went. I thought it was probably a tree in a

faraway forest. It would be a dream tree, and the branches would be filled with dozens of them, dark and warm and roosting. A child could fall asleep under that tree and wake up reborn.

Then my eyes would drift to the soft dusty yard, traced with their wing patterns.

A breeze would come, picking up to a brisk wind, and I knew by morning all those delicate patterns would be gone. The dust would be fresh again, like the smooth skin of a baby. So that when the men came out in the morning, they would tear no fabric, render no skin.

The soft-tufted night birds are like that. They are peaceful animals that want no harm.

It is amazing what we hear down here in the dungeon. The guards talk all day as they sit on their stools down the hall, watching us—watching a cellblock where nothing ever happens, where the doors rarely open. If they are lucky, once a week, they might chain a man to take him to the Dugdemona cage. The only way to fill the empty space and endless boring hours is with words.

They try to keep their voices down, but it never works. They talk and talk. The guards talk about the warden, about the lady—they can spend days talking about her and the priest—about the other guards and the budget and the hiring and promotions and corruption and dope and new inmates and everything else in between. It is like a pipeline of information to our cells.

Today the guards sound sad. It comes through in the morose clanking of their utility belts as they shift on the stools, in the bitterness underlying their voices.

"New shipment of men coming in," one of them says.

The other guard is silent for a moment. They both know what this means. We all know what it means.

"Tomorrow?"

"Yeah."

"More numbers," the first guard says, and you can hear his discomfort in how he shifts on the stool.

"Conroy will be happy," the other one whispers, almost too quiet to hear, but we all do, and the walls sigh with sadness.

The warden is thinking about the new shipment of men coming into general population when he sees the lady sitting patiently in the death penalty visiting room. The wood Dugdemona cage in front of her is empty. The lady sits in the chair, waiting for York. She sits very still, as if in waiting, her soul has left her.

The warden has come to tell her that the guards bringing York are running late. She looks up at him as he enters, his feet politely halting as he steps past the threshold. It is just the two of them, the lady and the warden, their eyes meeting.

For once he doesn't know what to say. "What, no attorneys?" he finally jokes.

She smiles. "I try to avoid them."

"Like wardens?" It is out of his mouth before he thinks twice.

Delight fills her face. "No, I always want to talk to you."

"That would be a mistake on my part," he says, coming toward her.

Suddenly he wants to talk to her, wants to face her, wants to ask her how she feels, trying to get killers off. Doesn't she care about what they did? Doesn't the reality of it ever bother her? Instead, he remarks of York, "The prince apparently woke up with his head on a pea called his ass."

She's not offended. "It's not like I would invite him to tea." She smiles.

He is standing close to her now. Close to the cage where she will talk to York, hunting for secrets to get him off the row.

"It's just a job to you," he says.

"It's not just a job to either of us."

"Aha."

"You like being the jailer," she says calmly.

"That I do. And you like being what?"

She stares up at him. With her short black hair and her gaze—so intense—she resembles a cat, a tiny, beautiful cat, born to hunt, to drive her prey from the woods. She is tougher than any convict, he thinks, harder than the men she frees from the row. She is more dangerous than all the killers combined because she is aware of what she does—and she chooses not to stop.

The smile vanishes and she just looks sad. Her eyes tell him she wishes it weren't so. But it is.

He thinks of the lady as he leaves work that evening, as the sunset illuminates the sky with gold shot through with streams of ocher. Everyone says *bye-warden, bye-warden*, as he makes his way through the locking doors. The words are like grooves on the stones. He waves to the female guard working the front tower, her rifle at the ready.

He is glad that women work here now. When he was younger and now starting in corrections, it was only men. The prison was harder and yet somehow weaker. Now the women put pictures of their kids up on their lockers and leave brownies in the lunch-room, but when they go on the rows, they go hard—and laugh while they do it. Even the hardest male convict wants a mom, he thinks, and these rough-and-ready women are ready for that role.

When he drives home, he tries to think of all the good things in his life. Fishing for sturgeon. Elk hunting in the woods. Baseball. His wife once accused him of being like all men by trying to make his life into a picture book and ignoring the next page.

None of the happy thoughts work. As always after he has talked to the lady, he is angry. She infuriates him in a way no one else ever has.

He has spent his life being the jailer. He knows he has his faults—he can be surprisingly naive for a warden. There are things that happen in the prison that he doesn't know about and doesn't want to know about. He is wise enough to know that as long as the wheel turns, a certain amount of dust gets thrown.

But after seeing the lady, he can't help getting angry. He takes his job seriously. Every day he protects inmates from one another and society from the inmates. It is not an easy task. He wants to tell the politicians to try policing three thousand men who spend their time trying to disembowel one another with shanks made out of sharpened table knives. Get back to me on how it goes.

And then the lady comes in and pulls a few tearjerkers for judges who have never stepped foot inside his prison, who have never met the victims or their families. And the next thing he knows, she is walking another man away from his deserved death.

It isn't that he minds when it is fair. There have been times when she walked guys and he was okay with it. He remembers one guy whom she got off. The guy had been convicted of murdering a drug dealer. The lady got him a new trial, and the jury decided it was self-defense. He himself walked that guy off the row and into freedom. He got heat for it later, but he stood by it. It was the right thing to do.

He knows there are too many black men on the row. He knows there are too many men who had Grim and Reaper for their defense attorneys. He tells his new guards there are more than enough guilty men to go around, we don't need to invent more. He is the first to admit the system needs fixing.

What he doesn't understand is helping the rape killers and serial killers and baby killers, the men like York and Striker and Arden.

When he thinks about what men like York and Striker and Arden have done, he is firm in his truth. Enough years of being the jailer—of seeing men kill one another in prison riots, of holding the hands of rape victims as they testify in front of parole boards—and he knows that some men deserve to die. He can chat with a man like York, he can even show kindness to a man like Arden, but he knows in his heart that they deserve to die. Such men are like diseased dogs or demented animals. You can bemoan what made them killers, but once they are, the best thing is to put them down with mercy.

Maybe, he thinks, the lady forgets about what these men did. She forgets that men like York hurt women, or men like Striker killed so many, and what Arden did is too horrifying to consider.

He stops himself. No, he thinks again, the lady does know those things. She talks to the men's families, she plumbs their lives, she has to know the pain they have caused. Yet she still tries to get them off, and this he cannot figure. This is the part that makes him mad.

He realizes with a start that he is home. The brown ranch lies at the end of a cul-de-sac in a neighborhood that is comfortingly monotonous. Black bugs whirl against the front door, and as dusk falls, the bats will whirl like brown darts from the trees, getting ready to celebrate the feast of the porch light.

As he parks in the driveway and opens the garage door, he sees a For Sale sign in the front yard. He blinks and the sign is gone.

It is only eight o'clock, but he knows his wife will be in bed. If he goes upstairs, there will be a ring of sweat in the tub and moisture on the curtain. Her medication holder will be on the counter beside a glass with melting ice and gin. With dullness, he will see the empty wig stand and the litter of pill bottles, an army accumulated against the enemy of cancer, which is winning.

He will go into the bedroom they have shared for twenty-two years, listening carefully for the tiny gasps of pain that will tell him what number she is today. Are you a four, dear? he wants to ask. I am a six, honey, he wishes he could tell her, just from the ache in my heart.

She will turn over in bed, hiding the pain and reaching for the wig at her bed stand. No matter how many times he tells her "I love you no matter what," she wears that damn ugly wig, even in bed. She will say, "Oh, honey, are you here?"

And he will say, "Yes, honey, I am."

The white-haired boy has a mouth like Cupid. The girls at school used to say his red lips were sexy. He rides in silence along with the others on the transport bus, nervously biting those red lips. He is only sixteen, but in our state, you can be judged as an adult even younger. It is not unusual for boys this young to be sentenced to our enchanted place.

The older, con-wise men on the prison bus look at the white-haired boy. Some look with sadness, others with appraisal.

The bus bumps down the prison road, under the watchtowers. The gates are slowly raised, and the bus pulls inside. The men are hustled off the bus. For some this will be the beginning of forever. They are not thinking about that. They are stiff from the long drive—the transport bus picks up new inmates from jails all over the state. They are bored and ready for their new life to commence, whatever it is.

The white-haired boy blinks in the sunlight, his chains dangling off slender arms, and the guards look at him and wince without knowing it. They know the score. Things happen in this enchanted place that no one can control.

The new men are quickly herded into a prison door. WELCOME TO THE STAT PRISON says a sign on the wall with crooked stick-on black letters under bolted glass. The E has fallen off and lies at the bottom of the frame. The men are ordered to sit. A guard moves along the row and takes off their shackles. The boy stares at the guard standing by a door and holding a rifle in his hands. The boy stares at the rifle. He realizes with a start that he has never seen a gun except for the ones on police officers and sheriffs.

When it comes his turn, the white-haired boy is called through the door. Inside a small concrete room waits a bored-looking guard wearing blue latex gloves.

"Undress," the guard says in a nasal voice. The boy quickly strips. The boy has the soft belly of youth. His tender penis has curled up into its nest of white hair. "Turn around." The boy turns. "Bend and spread." The boy bends and spreads. The guard only looks. "Turn and lift." He turns and lifts his penis. The guard reaches under his ball sack and feels with slippery-gloved fingers. "Dress."

The boy feels relief. That wasn't so bad. He picks his prison uniform from the large industrial laundry bins lined along the side of the room. Even the smallest size floats on him. But after months dressed in jail clothes, waiting for trial, the orange uniform feels like a relief to the white-haired boy. In jail, waiting for trial, he wasn't allowed shoes with laces. He laces his work shoes with satisfaction.

When they are all dressed, the new men are led down a hall into a large room. They sit in folding chairs and hold their new papers in their laps. It could be a classroom except for the bars on the windows.

"You came to prison as punishment, not for punishment," the guard at the head of the room tells them. "Make the most of it."

The new men are quickly led through the system. They are given a sheaf of papers: work assignments, cellblock assignments, a small manual of religious services, and a thicker manual of disciplinary rules.

The guard tells them if they have a problem to fill out a kite. The boy is confused until he realizes a kite is a complaint form. Each man is given a dozen.

Orientation is over. The white-haired boy is told to report to Cellblock G after free time in the yard for his cell assignment. He is surprised. He had thought he would be dragged to a cell and locked up. Instead, he and the others are let into the yard. The new men walk outside and look around the yard, and it seems the whole enchanted place stops for a moment and takes a breath. The guards stand rigid at the towers. When there are new arrivals, they are always like this. They scan the acclimation carefully.

Some of the new inmates who have done time before casually walk over to old buddies. Others head to the picnic tables in the shade to read their papers. The others stand there, confused. The shot callers at the weight pile study the incomers with smiles.

The white-haired boy feels sudden panic. He stands there, frozen. He is not sure what to do. How did I get here? he wonders. One day he was in math class, and then he was in jail, waiting for trial on auto theft charges. He knew what he did was stupid:

He and his buddies took a car for a joyride. Now he is here, sentenced to two years. When he was being sentenced, the judge told him this was his wake-up call.

The guards watch from their towers. The sky wheels above them.

The guard Conroy has deliberately guileless eyes. Watching him cross the yard, you might think, What an ordinary-looking man. From the slope of his belly over his service holster to the dust on his black dress shoes, there is nothing to distinguish him—until he turns his cold blue eyes on you. And then you think, Ordinary men can be more dangerous than any other.

Conroy works intelligence, which tells you enough. He wanders the yard, looking for the tallest trees. He knows them all by sight. Conroy likes the tall trees. He likes to stand in their shadows. It makes him feel powerful.

The tallest tree on the yard is a shot caller called Risk.

Risk has spent his time on the weight pile—so much that he looks like a steer on steroids. He has a tangle of long brown hair and a face scarred from fighting. He fell for opening up a drug mule with an X-Acto knife and then rummaging around his stomach for the balloons the mule had swallowed. This normally wouldn't get much attention, but in his case, the drug mule was his own five-year-old son. Apparently, by the time Risk was done, his boy looked like a piece of pink and white meat.

You would think a guy like Risk would be a pariah on the yard. But that is not the way it is inside. As much as I love books, I have never read one that tells what it is really like in a prison. In the books, the baby killers and rapists are hated inside prisons. That is not the truth. The truth is, it doesn't matter what you did on the outside. If you like to take it by force, if you want to beef up on the pile, you, too, can grow taller than the tallest tree in the forest. You can be the worst baby killer or rapist and still beat and rape your way into power inside.

What matters in prison is not who you are but what you want to become. This is the place of true imagination.

Cronies surround Risk. They are all huge guys grown into monsters on the weight pile and the extra food that comes with being shot callers. They have little kitchens in their cells, complete with battery-operated camp stoves. They dine in their cells on meals that would be unthinkable for the rest of us—gourmet concoctions made of the food sold in the prison commissary, where a candy bar costs five dollars. They cook packets of Top Ramen and mix them with huge chunks of cheese and cans of chili—chili with *real* meat—and they top these meals with real coffee and cream and sugar. The hot, delicious smells drift from their cell windows to drive the rest of the prisoners mad.

The shot callers are our kings. From their halls comes a constant supply of shanks, a regular prison industry where Risk will loan a blade for fifty dollars if he approves the death. They supply endless dime bags of heroin to the prison addicts, the tiny blobs of black tar wrapped in the crinkled wrappers from the candies left by the church women who come to pray and sob through their hands at the plight of these poor men—as a result, the heroin sold in here has been nicknamed starlight candy. The treasured few kits are kept in their cells, to be loaned for a steep price unless you are one of Risk's crew, and then you get to use the blood-spotted, dull syringe at no cost. They make fortunes out of selling pruno, the homemade alcohol grown in plastic bags and fed with bags of sugar, and for weeks their cell rows erupt with raucous, drunken laughter. They know that having too much money on their books is dangerous, so through corrupt guards, they send thousands of dollars in drug money to wives and girlfriends on the outside. All of this made possible because the guards don't turn their cells.

Conroy walks across the yard, the dust rising from his dress shoes and the medals on his regulation shirt gleaming. He comes up to Risk and slaps his shoulder. They walk off together, heads bowed. The whole yard sees the intelligence guard and the shot caller talking.

When they come back, both are laughing. Conroy grips Risk on the shoulder as if they are good buddies.

The entire enchanted place sighs with sadness.

The next day Risk saunters across the yard to the old black telephone hanging near the activities room. It is one of the few phones that is not recorded. Risk dials the extension by heart.

The phone rings in Conroy's office. Conroy calls it his yes telephone because when it rings, he picks it up and says one word: "Yes?" And then he listens. "The Norteños are bringing some black tar in through that dirty guard up front," Risk tells him. "The one that picks his teeth. They're dropping it for keister tomorrow. Enough fucking tar to pave this place twice."

Conroy hangs up the phone, and a loving smile wreathes his face. He knows exactly what to do. He will turn on the cameras in the visiting room and catch the guard accepting a package of black tar heroin—thousands of dollars of tar. He will catch the guard passing these bindles of heroin to one of the Norteño inmates working the visiting room. The camera will show the inmate going into the restroom with the package under his shirt, where he will tuck all of those bindles one by one up his works, in practice known as keistering.

Conroy will later show the incriminating video to the guard. The guard will grow pale and stammer. He knows this is not only a firing offense; it is a criminal offense. He could be convicted and thrown in here as an inmate. All the beatings he has given, all the twisted arms while cuffing, all the times he has walked away from the sounds of rape—those are the times that will be remembered by the other inmates if he returns as one of them. Nothing is despised more in our enchanted place than a castrated duck.

Conroy knows exactly how the guard will react. The guard will sweat and ask, "What do you want?"

After they negotiate, Conroy will pull the keistered inmate. He will take him down for a search and retrieve the bundles himself with his own probing hand. The Norteño gang member will say it was all his idea. He will refuse to name his leader. This is what Conroy wants. He will tell the inmate to tell the leader of the Norteños what it will cost to preserve that silence.

The inmate will go down for a short sentence, though he knows he will do easy time, cherished by his gang for his loyalty, and then advance up the chain. The teeth-picking guard will feel so much gratitude—and fear—toward Conroy that he'll give him a cut from now on for every drug deal he supervises. The addicted inmates will be happy as the flow of heroin inside our enchanted place continues, and everyone knows there are few other buffers to the raw edges of boredom inside. Every week the leader of the Norteños will leave an envelope filled with cash in Conroy's locker—another envelope to join the others, which is why Conroy has a fancy motorboat and a vacation home in the mountains while the warden goes home to a modest ranch and an old sailboat he never gets around to fixing.

The best part? Conroy will get written up with an official commendation for busting the inmate. It is one more rung on his way to the top. He wants the warden's job.

The bosses love him. There is no corruption on his watch.

In return for sharing this information, Risk gets his reward.

The next day the white-haired boy is rolled, with no warning, from his cell.

He was going to classes and making a few careful friends, even laughing at his work assignment in the clothing factory. His cellmate was an ancient

fart who snored too much but other than that was
harmless. Life was not that bad; he could begin to
imagine making it two years. After so much confusion and fear, hope was beginning to well up inside
him. Maybe he could finish school. Go to college,
even.

The guard at his cell door tells him brusquely
to gather his kit. Bewildered, the white-haired boy
quickly bundles his meager belongings—fresh
shirt, socks, and paperwork. The cell door slams
shut behind him while the old cellmate blinks his
rheumy eyes.

The guard walks him down the row. The cellblock grows quiet.

The white-haired boy has no idea where he is
going. Everyone else does. The whole prison knows
about the Norteño bust and Risk and Conroy's
clever hands. Everyone knows how this will end.

When the men see the white-haired boy walk
past, they turn away from the bars. Some go sit on
their bunks and don't say anything. Others smile a
little to themselves.

The white-haired boy is led across the dry,
empty yard to another building. The walls here are
older, the stone crumbling. He realizes this is Cellblock A—what the inmates call the Hall of the Lifers. No one does time here unless he's in for a long
time.

Deep underneath this building, the boy knows, is the dungeon of death row. The boy has never seen the death row inmates. No one in the prison ever sees them. They are trapped underground and never allowed up except for their brief trips to the Dug-demona cage, and even then they are led in chains down secret halls. The boy has heard their names—names like York and Striker and Arden—but he has no idea what they look like. They are the invisibles of the prison.

The men in the Hall of the Lifers stand up when they hear the hall doors slam. They come to their doors to watch the white-haired boy pass. The boy notices how big the men on this floor are, like caged gorillas. Their faces are masks. No one smiles at him or even nods. Their faces are blank.

The guard has stopped in front of a cell. The guard looks angry. The boy doesn't understand that the guard has been sent on this terrible mission and hates it.

The boy looks in the cell door and sees a man with a seamed face and long tangled hair. The man is lying on his back on his cot, his long hair flowing over his flat pillow. He stares at the ceiling as if he doesn't know the white-haired boy is there.

The door clangs open, and the white-haired boy is pushed inside.

Risk doesn't rise from his cot—not at first.

The cell coagulates with an acrid smell that the boy doesn't know but instantly recognizes. It is the smell of terror, and it is coming from him. Something like barbed wire constricts around his heart, and it is impossible to breathe. He knows now why he is here.

The kites float like origami birds, like paper snowflakes, floating and then raining from the cell door. They rain like passing thoughts on the floor, drift down into snow piles at the end of the corridor. *Please move me, please*, they say. *Please.*

There are prisons inside prisons, walls inside walls, and in this place you learn that your worst dungeon might be the room with the most windows. You can step behind one wall and then another here, like a child lost in a maze—and be lost forever.

There is no one like the lady for someone like the white-haired boy. That is the irony of prison. People like the lady are reserved for those sentenced to death. It is only when a man is sentenced to die that the faucets turn on and people start to care. The rest, like the white-haired boy, are erased.

So many complaint kites rain out of Risk's cell that they clog the walkway drains like rotting paper leaves. The men have to climb over the huge sodden piles on the way to mess, and they track pieces of paper that say *help* into the mess hall, where the wet papers roll into tubes that say *please* and are smeared into gray pulp on the floor on the men's boots that say *me*. This is the way it is, in this enchanted place.

In times like these, my cell seems dark for days. The air grows thick and I have trouble breathing. I follow the walls with my fingers, searching for the place in the stones that will let me out. I want out of the darkness, out of the pain and confusion.

Not even the books can save me in a time like this. I hold their pages to my face, and I howl inside that I cannot decipher their signals. It is all gibberish. And without this avenue out, my entire world comes crashing down.

Once in such a time, I slit my wrists with my teeth and rubbed my wrists on the walls like some crazy Manson killer. That didn't end well. The guards cursed and busted in my door and dragged me out by the hair to the infirmary. The infirmary is a place where they pipe in poisoned air, hoping you will die. No one wants to waste money on psychiatric medicine here, or cancer treatments, or any treatments. The taxpayers don't want to waste their money saving the lives of killers, and I don't blame them. The infirmary wards are filled with men yip-

ping with the late-stage pain of cancer or bleeding
through their bowels or raging in diabetic deliri-
ums. They kept me strapped to a table for days until
I got sores from the rubbing of my shoulders drumming the cot. I still have the scars on my shoulder
blades, like angel wings that never exploded.

Now when these dark times happen, I curl into
a ball on my cot and make a cape with my blanket.
I remind myself I am not dust, but I should be. I tell
myself I am made of the same cells as life itself even
if I am a mistake.

I pretend it is rain I hear, crying down the gut-
ters, and not the wet slap of flesh or the dark laughter in the cells of the Hall of Lifers far above me, or
the crying of a boy in pain.

The white-haired boy has been in the infirmary
twice, getting sewn up like a torn doll. When he appears to eat in the mess, he looks like someone broke
his limbs from the inside.

He never sits with Risk and his cronies. That
would be unthinkable. He sits with the other punks
at the worst table in the mess. The men at that table
are broken, and even the kindest among us treat
them like refuse. The white-haired boy sits with the
others as if he is not there. He stops talking. He eats
his mush and gray sponge meat in silence.

Days and weeks pass. And then one day a guard appears at the cell door. Without ceremony, he opens the door and gestures to the white-haired boy. When the boy looks at Risk as if to see if it is true, Risk doesn't look up from where he lies on his bunk.

Risk had his payment, and now the treat is over. Well, mostly over. The open playtime is over. Risk needs to make another call to the yes telephone if he wants another fresh cellie.

The white-haired boy cannot believe his luck. He bolts from the cell, too nervous even to gather his kit. With each step down the hall, the slick sweat of relief breaks out more on him. He can feel the rough stones again beneath his feet.

The same old ancient fart is in the cell, wheezing like nothing ever happened. The boy sits on his bunk in a sweaty daze. His whole body, his entire soul, hurts. It's over, he thinks. Thank God it is over.

But the next day he finds out it is never over.

He goes to mess like any other inmate. Only he isn't any other inmate, not anymore and never again. He could be transferred to another prison, and somehow they, too, would find out. It is amazing how the prison grapevine travels. He tries to carry his tray to a table where one of his shop classmates sits, and he is met with killer eyes. He turns to another table where everyone gives him the cold eye. Rebuffed, he backpedals. There is a moment of icy uncertainty as he stands in the middle of mess, the tray held in sweating hands. Finally, he walks forward to the only table he has known. The men there clear a place for him silently. Behind them, Risk and his crew laugh and turn away.

After lunch, the white-haired boy walks out on the yard. He doesn't know where to go. He goes to the baseball diamond and stands there for a while, watching a few guys enjoy the honor of playing with the only ball. They don't invite him to join. He walks around the track, stopping to look at the tiny corner of the yard where the old men are allowed to plant flowers. Even the old men ignore him.

The flowers are nice. The sun is out and it feels good. He begins to relax. He sits down at one of the picnic tables in the shade.

At that moment one of Risk's cronies strides over. He has a sunburned neck and huge shoulders straining his shirt. The sight of those shoulders makes the white-haired boy feel sick.

The big beef just looks at him like he doesn't deserve a smile. "Four o' clock," he says.

The white-haired boy looks back, dazed and uncomprehending. In the distance, Risk and his other cronies are bench-pressing at the weight pile, and the boy can hear the crash of metal plates across the yard. The men on the baseball field are peppering the ball. The old men are watering their flowers. The guards in the tower are looking to the sky.

The big beef points to a shed at the far end of the yard. The other inmates call this the rape shed. "Four o' clock," he says.

For Conroy, the matter ends well.

He likes the calls on the yes phone. He likes to pick up the cool handle, likes to hear the needy voice at the other end. He likes to say that first word. "Yes" is the most beautiful word in the world to him, a world of open doors and new adventures.

I hide under my cover when the trusty comes by. I can hear the creaking of his cart from down the hall, and the rustle of men excited. They call out for him, eager for contact, for voice, for the books and towels stacked on the old metal cafeteria cart used for everything around here. The men with money on their accounts get candy, soap, toothpaste, and if they are being good, razors. The rest of us get regulation toothbrushes, their handles snubbed, made by companies expressly for prisons, because the normal kind with long handles get sharpened into shanks.

When the trusty finally gets to my cell, he sighs. "Towel," he calls, and drops one through the slot. I peek and see him pick up my stiff used towel gingerly, as if it is poisoned.

I left my last book—a book about hiking the Cascades—out days ago, and I haven't had one since. I cross my scaly fingers under the cover that I will get a new book for this week. I hope it will be my favorite, *The White Dawn*.

"Book for you," he says, and my heart jumps. He talks almost unwillingly. "Warden says to tell you the library got a new donation."

The book drops with a soft thud. I can hear the trusty wait, like a boy at the circus, for the freak to show his face. He knows I want to rescue the book but cannot until he leaves. At last I hear the cart creak off and his ridiculing laugh. On the other side of me, he strikes up a conversation with York. Someone has put money on York's books—probably the lady, they say she does that sometimes—and he buys a candy bar. "It's my Payday!" York shouts, and men laugh on down the row. I can hear the rustle of wrapper and smell the peanuts from my cell.

I peek from under my cover. The coast is clear. I dive for the book. Only when back on my cot do I look to see what it is. Oh, joy. The trusty wasn't lying. It is a new book for me.

The cover is thick and made of red cloth worn thin. *Crazy Weather* it says. I stroke the cover and feel the vibration of the words inside. An old library sticker adorns the spine. AMITY SCHOOL LIBRARY in faded green print.

I open it to find an ancient checkout card tucked in a stained sleeve, and lift it reverentially. A boy named Charlie McBee last checked out this book. I smile at his childish scrawl.

And then I am inside the book, so much that I am only vaguely aware I have pulled back the cover for more light, and the trusty has wheeled his cart where he might see me, and I don't care. The world recedes. The little men with hammers in the walls curl into warm silent balls, and the golden horses far below lower their necks to listen. From very far away, I hear Striker whispering something to the trusty on his way down the row, and it seems odd enough to notice—why is Striker whispering? what is he asking for?—but then I am off.

I am off on a trip, in a different place than this, with a boy called South Boy and his Mojave friend Havek, and South Boy decides one morning to do a Great Thing. I can taste the sodden flapjacks the surly cook makes as I arise late in the desert heat, feel the warm slip of ditch water on my body.

If there are ever times when I would regret the choice York is making, it is times like these, when life feels like another page waiting to get turned.

The lady stands at a gate. It is a heavy metal gate with a thick padlock, the kind used to block logging roads. The gate has a large sign on it painted in crude black letters: NO TRESPASSING OR YOU WILL BE SHOT.

She is exhausted. She hasn't been home in days. It is now mid-June, and while she spends every working moment on this case, the days seem to be racing past faster and faster. She spent two days in the county seat, dredging up all the men she could find named Troy from the old microfiche census listings of Sawmill Falls. She narrowed her search to the key years of York's childhood, but there were more men named Troy—or TJ or JT—than she had expected. She spent another day in a motel room, living on greasy take-out food and working on her laptop to locate the men. Though some of the Troys are dead, a few are alive, spread out all over the county.

Now, after driving for hours through increasingly arid and empty country, she has found this gate. Behind it is one of the men named Troy, according to the last address she found.

The hills here are rugged, the forest dry with summer. Holly grows in the scrub. A faint thick, sweet smell comes wafting down the road. She takes a sniff. Yes, there is a sweet smell in these backwoods.

She hollers over the metal gate, her voice calling through the woods. "Hello? Hello?"

There is no answer besides an angry scrub jay. She tries to lean over the gate to see where the road goes, but it forks around a brushy turn and is gone.

His home could be around that corner. It could be miles farther up the road. He could be waiting with a sawed-off shotgun around that turn—she was warned, after all. She looks at the sign again and weighs the chance that she will be shot.

She has a choice to make, like always. She could turn back around on the dirt road and bounce her car for hours back to the city. Or she can climb over the gate and take her chances.

You knew there wasn't a choice, she thinks as she hikes her skirt and starts climbing.

Whenever the lady imagines what a person will be like, she is usually wrong. The doctor she might picture as a good man turns out to be a besotted worm. A priest she imagines would be rigid turns out lovably weak. A warden should be the enemy, but he is not.

And this Troy Harney, this man with a record of at least fifteen convictions for drug possession, disturbing the peace, and drunken brawling—this man she likes.

He answers the door with a quizzical smile on his grizzled face. He has been cooking a late lunch, and the small house smells like bacon and eggs. From the side yard comes the pungent smell of fresh wood shavings—he has been chopping wood for the winter and already has a large stack. The house has a warm, falling-down appearance, from the moss on the roof to a collection of abandoned boots near the front step.

"See you made it past the gate. You ain't selling Avon, are you?"

She smiles. "Gonna shoot me?"

He laughs, showing nicotine teeth. "Naw. That's for the police. Damn bastards. Come on in."

She explains who she is as she walks inside, but he doesn't appear concerned.

"How do you know I'm not the police?" she asks, curious.

He turns around and gives her a *my goodness* look. "Look at your shoes."

She looks down and smiles. She is wearing a pair of scuffed black boots with her skirt. "All right."

"You here for what again? Not often I get a pretty girl visiting me."

"I'm an investigator. I'm working a case involving a man on death row. I thought maybe you knew him. Or his mom."

Troy turns slowly from his little kitchen. Faded flowered curtains are pulled open around dusty-coated windows. Typical man, she thinks, not knowing how to clean.

"You mean Sawmill Falls." His face is sober.

"Yes."

He is quiet as he takes down two solid black plates from a cabinet. He spoons out limp bacon and scrambled eggs from a black cast-iron pan, then adds two slices of buttered white toast to each plate. "I always make extra," he mumbles. He pours a cup of coffee, adds sugar for himself, and pushes the bowl to her as he pours her a cup. "Sit."

They sit at a small wooden table with only one chair; he fetches a stool for himself. The cushion on the stool is faded with age and covered in yellow cat hair. He salts and peppers his eggs. Like a lot of men who live alone, he wolfs down his food, barely pausing to look up. "Eat."

She eats. The food is good, especially the eggs. "I put ketchup in them," he explains. "And a little bit of that garlic powder."

He waits until his plate is clear and scraped, and he looks a little longingly at her half-eaten plate. She smiles. "I had brothers growing up," she says, and once again feels the pang of the chameleon's truth as she pushes the plate to him.

He grins and begins stacking the eggs and bacon on her uneaten toast. "Makes a good sammitch. But you're waiting for me to talk."

"Only if you want."

He stretches his back. "If only the cops had someone like you. People like me would be dead in the water. You just sittin' there smilin'."

"No need to be hard."

"Sure. But I bet you can be."

Their eyes meet.

"I knew him. That man you must be working for. York. He was a boy back then." He pauses and studies a crust of bread. "That's who you're working for, right? You said death row and Sawmill Falls."

"Yes."

He wipes his plate with the crust. "Big news when he got caught."

"Were you still in Sawmill Falls?"

"Naw." He wipes the plate with his finger. "Left a long time before."

"Before?"

His eyes raise to her, slow and brown. "Yes, ma'am. Look. It wasn't easy."

"I know." She waits and drinks her coffee. "You knew Shirley, I bet."

He gets up abruptly and takes their plates. I screwed that up, she thinks. She watches him wash the plates—too hurriedly, with tepid water—and stack them on a bent brown dish drainer. She looks at his back in a brown shirt, the heavy jeans, and the worn boots. His arms are corded with muscle, though the slope of his shoulders tells her that he is a peaceful man. She remembers his record and thinks it is funny, how sometimes the men with the longest rap sheets are the safest. She worries more about the men too smart to get caught. He dries his hand with a faded dish towel. "Got to calve some more wood," he says.

"I never heard that phrase before."

"Grandpa used to say it. He was on them ships up in Alaska that went whaling. Came home and wouldn't stop talking about it. Used to say everything like it was whaling times." He chuckles. "We'd come up here to visit him and my grandma, and that's all the old fart would talk about. You'd think he hadn't married and had kids or nothing else but those damn whaling ships." He hangs his towel, his eyes faraway. "Want to go see my babies?"

"Sure," she says, and though she doesn't know exactly where he is going, she gets up and follows him out the back door. The old pasture is littered with broken-down wheelbarrows. She feels peaceful walking behind him, like a woods daughter behind her father. She developed a finely tuned sense of fear as a child—she knows when there is any danger. Her body tells her there is no danger in this man, at least now, so she can traipse after him through the sunny meadow and into the shady woods.

The sweet smell gets stronger as they zigzag down circuitous paths and scramble over logs set across dry creek beds. He lifts branches for her to pass under and, more than once, a string across the path—a poor man's booby trap, to see if others are spying.

"My grandpa left this land to me. When I left Sawmill, I came here. It took a lot of healing, I guess. I got into that hippie shit for a while, then some other stuff I won't mention. Mostly finding the bottom of the bottle. Looking for answers."

A spiderweb hits her in the face. She nonchalantly claws at her face and sees a huge orb spider hanging inches from her hand. Without a moment's hesitation, she claps both hands together and kills the spider, then wipes her messy hands on some ivy on a tree.

He grins with admiration. "Ain't afraid of bugs, is you."

"Grew up with too many."

"Human or fly?"

They come to an open clearing where the smell is intense. Dozens of huge pot plants stand at attention, reeking with the perfume of their potency. He breaks off a bud and rubs it between his fingers. "Pretty babies."

She waits. The smell is so strong, so female; she wonders if she can get high just from breathing.

He holds the tightly furled bud in his open palm. "I never got the whole thing, you know."

"With Shirley."

"With the whole town. It was like—something happened to us. Something wrong. And it was in me, too."

The smell is overpowering, but there is also the sky above, and the calm woods around, and she can see even in the fabric of his shirt that he does not want to hurt her. Like most of the people she sees, he has been waiting his whole life for someone to listen. "You said you left."

He nods. "I left because—I felt bad. I wanted to help Shirley. I moved in with her for a time, don't know if you heard that. Didn't just take from her like most of the men. But the other men, they had gotten used to it. They didn't want to back off."

"And York?"

"Oh. Oh boy. He was 'bout nine at that time, I suppose. He had these eyes—I can't explain. I tried to help."

"What did you do?"

"I brought stuff—food, mostly. I'd make them supper, feed that little boy. York's legs would hurt him something fierce, and I got this lotion to rub on them. But none of it . . . oh well."

She waits. The smell is dizzying, and Troy is framed in his pot plants.

"None of it worked," the lady says.

"No, ma'am. None of it worked. They kept coming even though they knew I was there—that she had a man now. They didn't care. They'd come when I was at work, and I'd get home and she'd be sitting on her bed, her legs all wet and that smile on her face. You got to see, ma'am, she was daft, okay? She was daft, and the men all knew it. They all took advantage of her, and oh my Lord, it was like something bad in all of us. I did it, too. I admit it, okay? But I—I cared about her. I wanted to help. She had some nice parts, ma'am. Did you know she had a pretty voice? She could sing like an angel." He is breathing heavily.

"York."

"That poor boy. Sometimes I'd get home and she would be just sitting on the bed, no pants, wearing nothing but an old blouse with flowers on it, with those wet naked legs. And York would be crouching in the corner. There wasn't no place, you see, that he couldn't see. There were times I thought the best thing I could have done was poke that boy's eyes out with a stick." He is still holding the green bud.

"They didn't just come for her, did they, Troy?"

His eyes are on her, beseeching. "No, ma'am. They didn't just come for her."

"I thought you were one of the men who hurt her. But you wanted to help."

"I didn't help her, ma'am. I tried and then ran like a chicken. I left that little boy. I left him and his mom to all those men. And later, when I heard what he did . . . I was a coward, ma'am."

"You promised York you would stay, didn't you?"

His face looks old, no longer handsome. "How did you know that?"

"A rabbit told me."

"Hey, crazy." Striker has been at his door for hours, whispering to me. "I know you can hear me, crazy man. I know you can talk."

I hide under the blanket on my cot. I climb against the bed wall and turn my face to the reassuring stone. I wish I had a book to hold, but I gave back *Crazy Weather* days ago. I read it three times first.

"Got something for you, crazy ass." Striker hoots like a monkey. His giggle is low and sharply melodic. A crumpled ball of stiff white paper lands in the hall in front of our cells.

I peek at the piece of crumpled paper from under my blanket. It looks like a page from a book. I am too far away to see if it has writing.

"See? Crazy ass. Here you go." Another ball of crumpled paper lands in the hall. "Want more? Crazy ass, it's what you get."

A distinct reek fills the row. It is the smell of shit,

ripe and pungent. I smell it often enough, from my cell and others. The toilets don't flush well down here, and the air barely circulates. But this smell is in front of me.

"I like your book, crazy ass."

Cold water fills me—cold water that turns to icy panic in my veins. I can barely hear someone on the other side of me say, "Aw, come on, knock it off, Striker." It is York, of all people, telling Striker to stop.

"You like the Eskimos, don't you? Crazy."

The sodden ball lands neatly in front of my cell. I can see the brown smears now, see the tiny print defaced with his shit.

"I heard you can talk, crazy ass. I heard you talked. You talked when you did him. Tell me about it, crazy ass. You're not fucking mute, you lying crazy ass. You can talk. Tell me."

A chorus of complaints is rising from cells down the row. It is not my book they are complaining about, it is the reek of fresh shit. I can barely hear them through my red rage. I begin to pull out my hair, tears smarting in my eyes. I remember what happened before I fell for the second time, and I am glad there are bars between Striker and me. Then I am not so glad, because I could easily kill him right now. I would strangle him and bash his ugly head against the stone floor until his skull broke and the brains and blood leaked from his ears and I would tear out his eyes with my long horny nails and I would use those sharp claws to tear open—

Another crumpled ball smeared with shit. It is the cover page of *The White Dawn*. "Let's hear you talk now, crazy ass."

It is too late. I am bolting across my cell, my hands up the smooth metal bars, ricocheting back soundlessly to bounce off the walls, tearing, ripping, banging against anything I can. There is a delighted hoot next door. I smash my arms against the toilet rim, rip holes in my cheeks, and spread the blood. Striker keeps hooting, laughing, and tossing the shit balls as he hears me smash around my cell. He knows I can make no sound, raging in my cell, and he rips and tears, and the entire row begins shouting, and yet no guards ever come until my favorite book lines the row in an ankle drift of shit-stormed paper. I tear my graying hair until it is lying in torn clumps on the floor, each clump a seaweed strand headed with little white follicles. My walls are smeared with my blood, which looks weak and watery even to me, and I ricochet off the walls again and again as I hear him laugh.

The warden comes two days later. I've been sitting with the blanket over my head. The trays have fallen willy-nilly on the floor, spilling untouched food.

"I heard what happened." The warden stands outside my cell. "Striker's an asshole."

They carried Striker off to the hole. It didn't have anything to do with me. The guards don't like shit. It has germs. When I first came here, one inmate shit-bombing another wasn't such a big deal, but now, with all the hepatitis and AIDS and staph infections, the guards get mad when someone shit-bombs another.

I keep my thin arms over my face under my blanket. I can feel the scabs starting to twitch where I tore out my hair. Now I know what it means when they say someone feels adrift, without moorings, when the most precious thing in life is gone.

The warden sighs. "People can be assholes sometimes."

There is nothing left.

"I bought something for you," the warden says.

The warden drops a small book with a white jacket through the slot. It is so new, I can smell the ink. The book falls as one stiff entity to the dirty stone floor. No pages flap, because the book has never been opened. The spine is unbroken.

I have never seen a brand-new book. I peer under the blanket through what remains of my raggedy hair.

The book has landed so the title is visible on the floor. *The White Dawn* it says.

I cannot help myself. I scramble off my bunk to rescue it. It cannot lie on the befouled floor. I grab it with long yellow nails. I hold it tight to my chest, feeling the stiff gloss of the cover under my fingertips. The smell of new paper and ink is like heaven.

My heart is beating, and now I know why they say beating like a drum. It is the drumming sound of blood running to all corners, flooding my body with the magic of the words inside. I scramble back on my cot and cover my head once again with the blanket, the book pressed against my thundering heart.

I want to tell the warden thank you, but of course I can't talk.

"How are you, Mom?"

This is what the lady always says when she visits her mom, and every time she says the word, it breaks her heart into pieces that she has to pick up in her hands and shove back in her chest.

Her mom has dried crumbs on her lips and a vacant look in her eyes until she realizes it is her daughter. The lady takes her mom's hand. It is cold, and she rubs it. Her mother wakes up to the world and starts complaining. This is what the aides say about her mom, too. She is a Grade A complainer.

Today her mom wants to complain about another resident at her disability home. She believes that the resident stole the perfume the lady gave her for Christmas, even though the aides have told her a million times that no one stole your perfume, you used it all up. But her mother is like that. She persev-erates, is the medical term, which is fancy talk for saying getting stuck in a hell of an annoying way.

The lady listens to her mom talk and talk and talk and feels the old dull ache inside her. This is her mother—the one who gave birth to her, pushed her from her canal. Breast-fed her, she was told, un-til she was almost two. Loved her, in her own way. Fed her when reminded, cuddled her when she cried. Forgot her at the park. Never knew how to take her to a doctor. Misunderstood thermometer readings. Called the ambulance for colds but let broken bones go untreated. Couldn't set an alarm clock so her daughter never got to school on time. Never bought a toothbrush or read her a book or cooked a recipe. But would hug and kiss her and loved her beyond all mea-sure. All the usual stuff of growing up with a mom with an IQ of 69, the lady thinks.

"Is everything okay, Mom?"

She has been her mom's caretaker since she was five. That was when she realized that her mom was one of them—a retard. The ones everyone made fun of. Even nice normal people on television make fun of retards. Short bus, 'tard, retard, she has heard them all.

She loved her mom anyhow. She wanted to protect her mom from the people who would make fun.
So she learned how to cook and clean. She took care
of her mother, and her mother's boyfriends took
care of her: a circle of sickness and despair.

She was never one of them—never one of the
normal people who teased and jeered and made fun
of her mom in the store, following behind them and
mocking her waddle-walk or the way she talked.
She didn't want to be one of her mother's friends,
either—the crazies and the slow learners and the
strange men who you thought cared even as they
shamed you. She could remember their names as
easily as she recalled the names of the men she knew
on the row. Danny, David, Alfonso. Robert and Joe.

Her mother seemed to wear an invisible beacon
when the lady was a child. Even a trip on the bus
could be a hazard—invariably, some creep would
want to sit next to the retarded woman and her
pretty daughter. How many times she had hope-
lessly tugged her mom's dirty sleeve only to be
shushed—you be quiet!—her mom thinking the
nice man wanted to talk to her, when it was really
the tiny dark-haired girl sitting next to her whom he
met with his gloaming eyes.

She realized early on that if she told anyone
what her mother let happen to her, they would take
her away from her mom. She was thirteen when she

told a school counselor, because she was afraid of getting pregnant. It was a day that haunts her still for the scalding sense of having failed her mother. When the police arrived at the school nurse's office to interview her, she looked in their sober faces and realized she was never going home again. She was sent to a foster home for sexually abused girls. Her only consolation was she was able to find her mother again, years later, and get her in this nice disability home.

"You okay, Mom?"

This is her mom, this woman with thinning hair and a squat body. This is her mom, with breath like ripe apples and breasts that lie unhammocked on her chest. A woman who let men come and go through her door for years, to molest her baby. Not out of evil but for a reason that's harder to accept: She didn't know better.

"I brought something for you," the lady gently says to her mom.

She pulls two Barbie dolls from her bag. Her mom always loved dolls. Her earliest memories as a toddler were playing Barbies with her mom. They would play for hours in the sun-splashed living room on the old ripped couch, under the shifting patterns of the torn tablecloth curtains. Finally, she would get hungry and go into their dank kitchen and climb on the counters to find something to eat.

Someone should have taken care of you, too, Mom.

She delights to see her mom's hazel eyes light up at the sight of the flaxen-haired plastic dolls. The two sit at the visiting room table and begin to play. An aide passes by, and a soft light comes into her eyes.

"Who are we today?" the lady asks her mother. She has an image of the priest sitting with them at the table. It is a surprising image but not a bad one. She thinks he would be kind.

"Princesses." Her mother giggles.

"Yes. Princesses," the lady says.

I sit in my cell and remember the psychiatrist I saw back when I was a kid, when they sent me to the mental hospital. I was maybe twelve at the time; I'm not sure, exactly. Time had stopped passing. I was safe. No one tried to make me talk.

The psychiatrist was young. He had blue eyes that were sunburned around the corners, and his hair was sun-bleached. He looked like a surfer. On his desk was a dried Play-Doh sculpture decorated with finger-paints. I thought maybe someday I could put a sculpture on his desk. He would brag about me to his friends. He would say my name and smile.

He didn't ask me to talk. He smiled and passed me a piece of paper. I took the stub of pencil he offered. I applied the pencil to paper and pressed as if my dreams were leaking out.

"Show me," he said.

I slowly drew a picture for him and silently handed it over.

He looked at the picture for a long time, and then he raised his eyes to me. The look he gave me was of infinite compassion. It was the first time anyone in my life had ever looked at me like that. Like he understood me.

"Where?" he asked.

I remember looking out his window to the freedom outside, out past the chain-link fence topped with barbed wire and the tiny plot of grass inside and the metal swing that no child ever rode.

I tapped my chest. It was inside me.

He nodded as if that made perfect sense.

He didn't ask the questions the others had asked, about why I didn't talk and what had happened to me and why I bit and growled and ran. He just sat back in his chair and looked at me for a long time.

I saw myself through his eyes. I saw a skinny boy with wild hands and wilder eyes.

"I wonder if we can help you," he said.

I shook my head.

His eyes met mine for a long time. Then we both looked out the window to the freedom we both knew I should never have.

The lady visits with York once a week now. She tells herself she doesn't have time; she should be working nonstop on his case. But she promised to build him a castle, the safe place he needs to tell his secrets, just like all the other clients. He may even change his mind.

Today the sun is weak and honey-colored. York smiles at it with his funny-notched teeth. He doesn't care about what she has been doing on his case. He wants to talk about himself.

He speaks of the little things that are coming back to him. "It's funny how being close to death helps you remember," he says. "There was this school bus would come pick up all the kids in Sawmill Falls to take them to the school in Squiggle Creek." He tells how he would wait for the bus outside the shack where he lived with his mom at the end of a dirt road. Sometimes the bus came, but most of the time it did not. He talks about a teacher who taught him how to count using dots. He talks about Auntie Beth and how she cooked a mean fried chicken on that old black stove back in the day. "Hell of a cook," he says, and the lady wonders how much of this was imagination born of hunger.

He talks about his mother. "She was a good mom," he says defensively.

The lady nods. "She loved you," she says simply.

"Yeah. People don't get that."

"Why not?"

"Because—you know."

"Love isn't stopped by illness," the lady says gently. "Not yours or hers."

York gives her a startled glance and then nods. He is close now.

"She tried—she did," the lady says, so softly. "She couldn't. But she loved you. And you loved her. No matter what you did later."

His eyes are growing darker.

"The ones who came to visit—they didn't love your mom."

Now she sees the rage. It is right there, behind the glittering eyes.

York begins speaking in a low voice. It is a voice that reminds her of birds that sing after dark.

"I got older, you know, puberty, and it was like electric flashes went off in my head," he says. "I had these—strange currents."

"Yes."

"It started when I was about twelve. I had been

eating dirt—I was hungry, okay—and I thought maybe a strange walnut seed had planted itself inside me, you know, right inside me above my parts. I thought maybe the walnut had sprouted."

She has to be so careful, each step. "What did the walnut seed become, York?"

He looks anguished. "A hard tree that wanted to push and push."

She bows her head, listening. Storms blow through her. What is it in our world that breeds such howling despair?

"Lots of times I go to sleep and think tomorrow will be the day I wake up and feel sorry," York remarks. "But when I wake up, I never feel sorry."

She raises her damp eyes. "Could you?"

"How would it matter?"

She thinks how the attorneys who hire her don't understand. They don't understand that men like York were damaged long before they got here, damaged by what they did, then damaged by years spent living in the isolation of the dungeon. The attorneys think that getting them off death row will turn these damaged creatures into walking, talking real people with rounded edges—real people who can take a deep breath that doesn't hurt their soul.

Men like York are like the sightless fish that live

in caves deep underground. Hauled above, they will perish.

"I understand why you want to die," she tells York.

"Most people say that," he says.

"I'm not talking about living on death row," she says. "I meant I would want to die if I were you."

He stares at her. There is heat in his hawk eyes. "Yeah? Why? Because of what I did?"

"Yes."

The anger in his eyes passes and is replaced with sadness. "I don't like having to be nice, especially to a pretty lady like you, but I'm willing to do it this once. I'll ask you please."

"Please what?"

"Walk on out of here and let me die."

When a man like York says he feels no remorse, I believe him. How can men like us really know what that word means? We hunt around inside ourselves like squirrels trying to find nuts, picking up each emotion and asking ourselves, "Is this remorse? Is this guilt?"

Men who have not been violated don't understand what it is like to have the edges of your body blurred—to feel that every inch of your skin is a place where fingers can press, that every hole and orifice is a place where others can put parts of their bodies. When your body stops being corporeal, your soul has no place to go, so it finds the next window to escape.

My soul left me when I was six. It flew away past a flapping curtain over a window. I ran after it, but it never came back. It left me alone on wet stinking mattresses. It left me alone in the choking dark. It took my tongue, my heart, and my mind.

When you don't have a soul, the ideas inside you become terrible things. They grow unchecked, like malignant monsters. You cry in the night because you know the ideas are wrong—you know because people have *told* you that—and yet none of it does any good. The ideas are free to grow. There is no soul inside you to stop them.

When I left the state mental hospital at eighteen and the wind chased the papers from my hands and I walked until I found that house, I thought maybe my soul was hiding behind the fluttering cloth over the window.

My soul was not there. The ideas were there, and the ideas hatched into something too terrible to name.

I had good attorneys, even for back then. They were not like Grim and Reaper. They hired a man who had the same job as the lady. The man brought in witnesses. Some of the jurors cried. I listened to the witnesses—the social workers, the neighbors, even my grandparents, looking so very old and sad—through a veil of hair. The newspapers said I was without emotion. How could I have emotion, hearing my life played backward?

When the jurors came back and said no death, the attorneys slapped me on the back, while behind me, I heard a woman groan. The attorneys said a life sentence was unheard of in cases like mine.

The attorneys seemed ecstatic, but they were not going where I was going. I had been handed a bomb to carry for the rest of my life. The bomb was my life.

The attorneys for whom the lady works have a private firm. They have a nice table in a conference room. They have a secretary to answer the phone. There are enough honors and plaques and awards on the walls—many from the cases she worked on—to make your head spin.

They have everything but common sense, she thinks.

The attorneys refuse to believe that York genuinely wants to die. They refuse to discuss whether he has a right to consider it. They've been arguing about it for close to an hour.

"He is not changing his mind," she says.

"How do you know that?" asks the younger attorney somewhat belligerently.

She takes a sip of her coffee and calms her voice. "I've been pushing him lots of different ways. I even told him I'd want to kill myself, too, if I were him."

"You told him what?"

"But I get nothing. He reacts a little, and then poof. It's gone."

"He's committed," the older attorney says thoughtfully.

She gives him a grateful glance. "Not just committed," she says. "If he were just committed to dying, we could try to change that—make him get committed to living. No. This is something different."

"What is it?" he asks her, and she can see the respect in his eyes.

She pauses. "He's ready."

The older attorney winces. The younger one just looks truculent. He changes the subject. "How is the work going?" he asks her.

"Well enough," she replies evasively.

"Finding anything?"

She thinks of York's mom, sitting on her bed in a flowered blouse with her bare wet legs. She doesn't feel like talking about it. She drinks her coffee and doesn't reply.

"We only have a few more weeks," he adds, as if she doesn't know this. She takes another sip.

The two men let it go. They trust that if something is there, she will find it.

As she leaves the office, the older attorney puts a hand on her arm to gently stop her. She turns and sees the interest in his eyes. The lines of care etched around his eyes tell her it is a warm interest, a nice interest.

She can't go there anymore. She has before, and it never works.

The building that scares me the most is Cellblock H.

I don't like to even think of it, a cold white building in the middle of our warm beige stone. Our stone walls are alive, but Cellblock H was made out of cold concrete, built during the 1960s by men representing all the advances in modern mental health science. The walls are spackled smooth. There are no windows in Cellblock H, not even the narrow windows with bars like the other men have in the other cellblocks. That no one cut windows is like God deciding a body doesn't need to breathe. It is a building without a throat. Men go in there and never come out.

The officials call it the Intensive Management Unit. The inmates call it the death house. The crazy men—well, crazy in a way that annoys the guards—get sent to Cellblock H. If you are quietly crazy here, no one minds. Cellblock H is supposed to provide all the best in care. The orderlies don't wear uniforms, and guards don't strap guns. Air-conditioning whisks away all bad smells, and soundproof walls silence even the loudest screams.

The cells are tight boxes of solid metal, including the doors. There is a narrow slot for the meal trays, but it's closed between feedings with a soundproof metal hinge. When a man is locked inside one of these metal boxes, no one can hear him scream. An inmate can stay in those metal cells for days, for weeks, for years. No one knows or keeps track. Only a clipboard hanging outside tells the guard who is in the box and when the inmate was last fed. If the clipboard gets dropped or someone takes it away to make copies, it might never get returned. Then the man inside the box is truly alone.

Once years ago the guards noticed a bad smell coming from one of the metal cells at the end of tier one. It was a cell they thought had been empty. There was no clipboard, so there was no reason to believe the cell was occupied. When they opened it, they found a man who had died weeks before. The constant air-conditioning had whisked away most of the smell and preserved what was left of his hands. He had gotten so hungry, he had eaten off his fingers.

There was an investigation, like there always is. The lost clipboard was found; it had been buried in a laundry bin. The inmate had been the head of one of the prison gangs. There was some confusion over why he was in Cellblock H in the first place. There were whispers that a rival gang leader and a corrupt intelligence officer had set it up. The confusion was so great that the investigators threw up their hands and called it a regrettable mistake.

The little men with hammers are inside the walls of my cell.

I'm not sure how they get here so quickly. One minute the walls are silent and the next they are there, sometimes in force. They have a very distinctive smell, like wet sawdust and urine. They scamper through tunnels under the yard and under the buildings like gophers, until all of a sudden they pop up here, dozens of them. You'd think the walls would be tight. No. This place is pockmarked with holes and secret tunnels.

I hear them sneaking late at night in the wall behind my cot. I'm sure the warden sent them. No, I think. The warden is okay. He wouldn't do that. So who sent them?

I slide along the wall and press my ear to it like a stone spider, breathing softly in the dark.

The men scamper and giggle so softly. They snicker in low voices, as if they are having a real party in there. I can never make out exactly what they are saying. I have the dreaded fear that they are climbing to the ceiling to make it collapse. All the collected weight of the earth above will fall on us. It is a clever plan. We will die choking on dirt and dust. That's okay for me, but I don't like the idea of them doing that to the others. Well, they can kill Striker, but not the others.

"Don't do it!" I want to scream at the little men. "Don't tear down the walls!"

Of course, I can't talk. I can only huddle on my cot, miserable. I grind my teeth so hard that sharp pains explode along my exposed nerve endings. I listen to the scampering so long, I finally spit out one of my few remaining teeth. It lands on my lap, a long bloody yellow tooth crowned with black.

Hours later, the small men finally fall silent. I want to sleep but cannot. My jaw aches.

I don't trust them. What did they do? Why were they here?

I realize it now. They have strung a black whirling cord through the walls, and when they leave, they will push the start button and the phone recorder will play.

Please don't do this, I want to whisper. *Please don't.*

The little men don't care about me. I am just one of the cordwood bodies they scamper over deep in the night, eating the dead skins off the soles of our feet.

Is that a dial tone?

No. I fall back on my cot. A phone is ringing in a distant land. I put my pillow over my face and scream silently inside. I can hear it still.

A trembling female voice on the other line is answering. "Donald?" says the voice once again. "Donald?"

The lady and the priest are walking the grounds outside the prison, under the shadows of the cyclone-barbed walls.

They walk under the shady elms and step over the green spiny creatures under the walnut trees as though they are alive. The priest walks slowly, as if dragging his feet. The lady walks like a forest sprite waiting to find what is exciting around the next corner.

"Most Catholics would say you are doing God's work by saving lives," the priest offers hopefully.

She shakes her head. "I'm not saving any lives. I'm only ending a few executions."

"Is there a difference?"

She glances at him. He knows there is a difference. She looks at the high wall next to them. "There are almost a dozen men in there I've walked off the row. They won't die of execution. But I can't say I've saved their lives." She pauses. "I can only say I postponed their death."

His eyes soak up the clean look of her skin, the darkness of her eyes. "For a lot of people, that would be enough."

"To live like that? I'm not sure."

"Most of the men you've freed are happy to be in there," he says.

She shakes her head. "What does that say about us or about them?"

He stops under an elm tree. A light wind shakes the leaves above them. July is around the corner, the red circle racing forward. The lady feels the press of panic. She shouldn't be here, talking, when York's execution date looms.

"Would you save them all?" he asks.

She knows he is asking about himself. "Yes."

"Even someone like Arden?"

The lady considers what she has heard about Arden—about what he did, or as close as her mind will allow before it skitters away in horror. She thinks about how sad it is that we remember the killers and not their victims. What if the world forgot Hitler and remembered all the names of his victims? What if we immortalized the victims?

The breeze lifts the hair above his brow, and he waits for an answer.

"I would save Arden," she says.

He nods, and they walk some more as if there is nothing left to say.

The lady has a sick feeling in her stomach. She feels like she has confessed a terrible sin, the sin of her willingness. But the priest feels a lifting of his entire soul. If she would save Arden, he thinks, she might save me.

The lady is debating in her head with the attorneys, since she doesn't want to do it in person.

She is asking attorney A, the little snot, about giving York some medical tests. Can she ethically ask him to do it without really explaining why? The younger attorney starts talking, and right away she knows this is going nowhere.

She hears attorney B, the older and wiser one, saying no, no, listen to the lady, she knows her shit. Then attorney B starts talking some law stuff that sounds like logarithms from hell.

She decides to deal with it herself. She is feeling

oddly secretive about this case. She doesn't want the attorneys to know what she is doing just yet.

The answer is as easy as a phone call to a medical expert she knows: A vial of blood is all he needs. He'll get back to her within a few days.

The lady slowly walks the dungeon rows. She says their names to herself as she passes each cell. Jones, Hildebrand, Sandoval, Large, Hall. Junior, Martin, Pearson, Lockridge. Mayfield, Porter, Aguilar, Flack, Green.

The men look out at her behind bars. Ratcliff, Hoffman, Leopold, Mason, Curtis, Rogers, Dowd, Duncan, and Wyatt. Some of the men put their hands between the bars, as if pleading for help.

Boon, Watt, Hurley, Saltzman. Jeffries—he's scheduled soon, after Striker and York. He looks up at her from his bunk. She can see he is resigned.

She looks inside each cell, meeting their solemn eyes. Wincour, Casey, Williams, Caird, Irvin, McLear, Graham, Becker.

There is one cell she never tries to peer inside: Arden's. She walks faster as she passes Arden's cell—something about it emanates a horror that scares even her.

Sutro, Hakim, Dupree, Holt, Shaw. She breathes easier.

The warden is watching her from the end of the

row. He stands alone, swinging the big old-fashioned ring key. He has looked much older recently, she notices, and she feels a pang of sympathy. She has heard about his wife's having late-stage cancer.

"Deciding which guy to take next?" he asks her.

"I have a waiting list," she quips.

He leans his head back and roars, a clean, bright laugh that shakes off the bars and surprises both of them. He has nice teeth, she notices. His shirt is unbuttoned at the top collar, and she can see silver tufts in his black chest hair.

"Oh my. Well, take your time. We won't be waiting around for you."

"I know." She smiles and steps around him.

She finds the priest in his office. His head is bent over a book, and the lamp catches the bald spot on top of his head. Precious little spot, she thinks. He looks up, startled. A pink flush catches his cheeks.

"I'm sorry," she says.

"It's okay. I was reading—this," he says, and turns the book so she can see the title. *The White Dawn: An Eskimo Saga*, by James Houston.

Word was out about Striker defacing a copy of the book. The priest thumbs the pages. "I was hoping if I read it, I could understand why it means so much. And if I can understand that, maybe I can understand these men." He puts down the book. "But it just seems like a story." He trails off, the pink still in his cheeks.

She feels a wave of protection toward him, to be so uncertain in his grown-man body. "If you understand what makes him tick—what is magic for him—then you can understand anyone," she says.

"Yes. But I wasn't thinking of the word 'magic.'"

"It's magic," she says.

"The church has funny positions on magic."

She shrugs, her shoulders thin under a warm blazer. It is always cold down here in the dungeon.

"I'm not talking black magic or even magic-magic," she says. "Not potions or prophecy or punishment." She stops and searches for the words, unconsciously leaning against his desk with one hip. He looks up at her, sees the feathery black hair framing her delicate pale face while she thinks. "I'm saying hopeful magic. I don't know this inmate. But I imagine he knows magic, if he is reading books. The book itself doesn't matter. It's that he found another world in it." She looks down at the priest. His mouth is slightly ajar. "Men like York, like Striker. Even men like Arden. They can see the magic just like us," she tells him. "No matter what they did, they can see the magic. I think your God would understand that. He may send them to the fires of hell, but he would understand that their eyes can be the same as ours."

"And their souls?"

She takes a breath.

"I'm sorry," he says automatically.

"Don't apologize." She smiles and collects her thoughts and shifts her body to accommodate them. Her small hand lands near his larger hand on the desk. "I don't know," she finally says. "What is a soul?"

"Is it your magic?" he asks.

"It could be." She smiles and, without thinking, touches his hand.

The touch lies there. The warm current is back, a sense of connection for her—a connection she has rarely felt with another person. They let the moment lie and absorb, and she is thankful that he doesn't pull away from it or make amends or explain it. He just seems okay with it, and that fills her heart with pleasure.

She is almost regretful now about what she has come to do. But she will do it anyhow, because it is her job and her client. She gently pulls away her hand.

She takes out a small syringe she has hidden in her inside jacket pocket. She knew it would pass the metal detectors. It is the standard plastic needle and syringe used by diabetics and drug users alike, sold by the weight in drug supply houses and supplied free on the streets for heroin addicts, in hopes of reducing nasty diseases. She got this one in five minutes by stopping at a pharmacy.

The priest looks at the syringe in her hand. She can tell he is thinking: Have I been played? But he knows that he has not, that she came on this mission and found something else. For once he feels he understands.

"I need some blood from York," she says. "I need you to go to him and ask him to fill this syringe. Then I need you to cap it and return it to me as soon as possible."

"I don't know how to take blood."

"You don't have to. York will know. He's been in prison for years. He's got a high H number."

"Come again?"

She smiles. "Prison slang for doing heroin. This is a dirty prison, by the way. Heroin addicts want to get sent here because the supply is so good. York will know how to pull his own blood. Oh, and please wear gloves when you touch it."

The priest looks at her sad dark eyes. "What do I tell him?"

"The truth. That the lady wants his blood."

"What if he says no?"

"He won't."

"Why not?"

She reaches back into her bag and pulls out a photograph she took of Troy Harney at the end of her visit. It was full dark by then, and the woods outside were covered in blackness. Troy had invited her to stay, but she had demurred, feeling the heat of his loneliness. She didn't want to deal with a man climbing in her bed, even a polite man who would listen to no. So she had said sorry, but please, let me take your picture right here in the kitchen. Troy Harney had obliged, and here was this picture of him, his brown eyes caught red in the flash.

"Tell him I found Troy."

"Troy?"

"He'll know when he sees the picture. Tell him— tell him there is more than one way to have a party."

The next day the priest discreetly walks by her as she is rushing to leave the prison. He hands her a manila envelope containing the syringe. She is distracted, trying to leave the prison as a lockdown is going into effect, and she barely has time to say thank you. She escapes the slamming doors moments before the red lights flash and the whole place slams shut.

She peeks inside the envelope when she gets to her car. The syringe is full, the outside smeared with blood. Hopefully, the priest wore gloves. A man like York is bound to be a hot pot of hepatitis.

There is a little note penned in the illiterate block writing of the uneducated.

TROY LAST NAME? York's note asks.

You little shit, she thinks. Plotting from death row to hurt the only man who wanted to help you. I'm not telling you his last name, not now or ever.

The next morning she sends the syringe to her friend the doctor on a rush order.

To get to the top of the guard tower, you first unlock a heavy door. Then you climb the narrow, musty stairs. The stairs rise above you into a dim and cavernous future. You go up, flashlight and baton and gun and regulation knife clanking, carrying your rifle in one hand, your accordion lunch box in the other. Your black utility belt is heavy. If there were a fire, there would be no way out, and you would roast here because the fire department leaves this enchanted place alone. You think this is what it was like, climbing the stairs of a turret in a castle or a dungeon so many centuries ago.

When you get to the top, there is no lady-in-waiting. There is only you in a small room shaped like a lighthouse. You put your rifle down on the desk under one of the open windows. From your spot, you see the next guard tower, and you wave at the guy. You leave your lunch box next to the radio, which you tune to your favorite country radio station, lightly, because you know the bosses frown on loud radio. The radio helps you get lost in reveries of happier places and times. You have to keep the radio low so you can hear the noise calling off the yard—how annoying it is to hear the same voices every day, the shot callers, the pleasers, and the blowhards.

You take your seat at the open window. You put your rifle on your lap. You look over at your friend at the next tower, and then at the wide open sky. You can see the river that winds next to the prison on the other side of the wall. The scene outside is peaceful; the prison is set away from the town. Outside of the asphalt parking lot, where you can see the hood of your truck reflecting the blinding sun, there is no sign of civilization. Only the rolling hills.

The radio is softly playing. It's a nice song that makes you think of swimming in the local creek when you were a kid. Down in the yard there is the crash of the weight pile and the endless hustle of bragging words. The big blue sky keeps the inmates contained, like flies in a bottle. They have no idea how small they are.

The worst part of being in the tower is the boredom. Hours of boredom, of hearing the voices and the weight pile and usual jeers—hey, Tommy, got that dope, hey Joe, what's an ass like you doing in here—and all the time you know that at any moment all hell can break loose. Without warning, the yard can erupt in riot, like one of those zombie movies where the infection spreads and suddenly they are all arms out, blood and teeth and slaughtering and bloodshed.

So you start looking for the signs. You watch for the one inmate standing with his arms crossed, a careful look on his face. You look for new movements at the weight pile, or a solitary man striding across the yard in a direction he should not be heading. Sometimes it is the soft thud of the ball being thrown and then a player turning all of a sudden, rage etched on his face.

Most often it is the days when a new cat comes on the yard. The worst new cats are the famous killers. It doesn't matter what they are famous for: It is the fame and not the crime that is the infection among disenfranchised men. The more famous, the more infectious they become. Those are the days you watch. You have already heard. Daniel Trubock, the famous wife killer, is coming into the yard today, if he dares.

He dares. You see his red hair cautiously coming out the orientation doors, bobbing uncertainly, and you see the inmates around him pause and then recede like waves at low tide. The big beefs at the weight pile turn and watch. You are not worried about them—men like Risk will take their time with men like Daniel Trubock. Right now they are just going to watch with sick grins. What you are looking for is the youngbloods, the hot young men wanting to make a name for themselves.

You stand up and hold your rifle, your hands calm. Your heart is fast but steady. All the rules say: It is okay to shoot. You know it in your heart, too. It is okay to shoot. The men below are small, and the infection spreads. If it spreads too far, too fast, it will get out of control before you can stop it, and then you have those terrible times when prisons riot and the smoke rises and guards like you are held hostage and tortured and dismembered and killed. It has happened here, you know, and you know it will someday happen again. You do not want to be one of those guards with your legs and arms strewn across the yard.

You lift your rifle like you do now, to your shoulder. You watch the little bobbing red head and pray you will not have to do this even as your heart hardens to it. The illness is spreading around your heart. You don't want to. But you will, and when the infection spreads—you can feel it all of a sudden in the movement of the yard and the parting of the men as one guy cuts to the left and heads straight at Daniel Trubock, so fast it takes your breath away—then you know you have less than seconds to make a decision whether the flash you see in the running man's hands is a shank or just the sun in your eyes.

You know in your heart what you will do. It will not be the attacker you shoot. It will be that little bobbing red head in the middle. That is the one your heart tells your finger to want—to get rid of the infection in your midst.

The fallen priest comes down the row. I can hear in his footsteps that he doesn't like what he has to do today. It has to do with Striker.

The guards are waiting outside Striker's cell. "Number six," the priest mutters, "number six I have shepherded to death this year."

The priest's lean body remembers the robes, but his shoulders have shrunk in refusal. Now he wears khaki trousers as if he picked them off a rack at random, and they hang on him as if they belong on a different person. He looks like he has lost weight all these months, serving a diet of death.

The guards hate the priest. To them, men like the priest paper the sky with romantic tissue-paper legends, but down here below the earth, in this enchanted place, we know life cannot be contained on a slogan or a prayer tablet. We know that kindness rules with the fist and chains rule with a turn to the sky, that all humans require penance and without it we all seek punishment, over and over again, until the body and mind are satisfied and we die.

We can hear the meagerness in his voice, the near whisper as he gets close to the cell and asks admittance. The little men with hammers sit back on their haunches deep in the walls and listen, chattering in happy gossip with one another.

I hear the fear in the voice of Striker as he responds. It is the fear of a man about to meet his death.

The doors clang open and the priest goes inside, accompanied by guards.

I hear Striker weeping.

The priest cannot administer last rites because he is fallen. But the soon-to-be-dead don't care. Striker asks the priest for a prayer, and I hear the priest's soft, melodic voice before I begin to fade into memories.

I hear music in my head, which is funny, because it is a song I have not remembered in so many years. It is a song that played on *Lawrence Welk* when I was a child. I remember now—I was staying with my grandparents. They had a home by the bay, out past the oyster beds. I must have been about eight, maybe a year before I was taken away. Isn't it funny how, as you get older, some early memories come back? That is happening more often to me, as if memories of the outside are returning and this enchanted place is turning into the dream. I remember how the surf crashed against the wet rocks of the wild bay, and how my grandparents had a little weather-beaten house on the shore. I can see my grandpa's red lobster hands, scarred from fishing. I remember thinking the sea was smoking from the spray it threw, and the wild seal smell of the rocks. My grandpa had told me that seals bobbed in the waves, and I stood for hours on the wet rocks that day, watching for them, thinking of their smooth, glossy brown fur, their plump bodies and large wet ebony eyes.

That night my grandmother gave me a bath, weeping silently while she scrubbed me, and she dressed me in pajamas that stuck to my damp back. I sat in front of their little television, waiting for my favorite song from *Lawrence Welk*. It was the song at the end of the show that I loved—the goodbye song. I heard it now as Striker wept.

> *Good night, good night until we meet again*
> *Adios, au revoir, auf Wiedersehen, till then . . .*
> *Good night, sleep tight . . .*

Isn't it funny how you remember? I remember my grandmother bringing me a mug of homemade hot chocolate, so hot the marshmallows seared

my mouth, and a heel of fresh-baked white bread
smeared with margarine. I ate my sweetie snack and
she took me to bed and tucked me in, and I listened
as the surf crashed against the rock, hearing the
sweetness of that goodbye song as she and Grandpa
talked in low voices in the bedroom next to mine.

"He could talk before, Eldridge," she whispered.

"I know, Mother, I know," my grandfather re-
sponded.

The next day I was wearing the same clothes I
had worn the day before—my only clothes, now
washed and pressed, the faded orange pants
two inches too short and the shirt frayed at the
buttonholes—and my grandmother's face was red
with tears, and I was waiting to get picked up by
my mother and her new boyfriend. No matter how
much I knew it hurt my grandmother, my heart was
bursting with hope, and I couldn't wait to dart out
the door because I loved my mom and always would.

"I know, I know," I hear the priest saying now.

The entire row has fallen silent to listen.

"Is it too late?" Striker begs.

The priest doesn't answer. His heart is pale with
practice. He can no longer lie. "God will tell you the
answer," he says quietly.

The row is quiet. On the other side of me, York
sits in his cell and listens, his hands quiet in his lap.

I sit on my cot, the blanket over my head, clutching *The White Dawn* to my chest.

This is the way it is, every time, all the time. Other people have doors to shut, rooms to cross. Here we have no privacy. We are trapped, naked to one another at all times. Every shit, every fart, every snore, and every cry in the night—we hear it all. Our doors must be fashioned out of desire. But maybe doors made of wishes are stronger than steel.

The prayers are done. The priest rises, sweaty, feeling as always that he didn't do it right. God would like him better if he were better. Please Lord, he thinks, let me be better.

Striker wipes his face. He hunts for a sense of absolution in himself and turns to the priest as the man shakes out his sweaty trousers. "Is that all?" he asks.

The priest nods. Yes. That is all.

"I thought it would be more."

The warden is at his cell door, flanked by guards. The guards are wearing the special black shirts of the executioners. The warden is dressed as he always dresses, in slacks and a dress shirt.

The warden doesn't like to drag these things out. "Done?" he asks the priest deferentially.

The priest nods. He wishes the lady had been on this case. But Striker was not her client.

Striker is crying. "I don't want to die," he sobs.

That's what you get, I think, for destroying my book, you bastard. I hope they mess up the medicine and you choke on your way to hell.

"Ready?" the warden asks him, and I hear Striker gasp yes.

The door clangs open, and I hear the black shirt guards enter to chain Striker in leg chains and cuffs.

Striker is silent as he shuffles out of his cell. Jesus made a last walk, I think, and so did Hitler. We all get a turn, and now it is yours. The only one we've missed so far is the devil, and once we get him, you and me is out of business.

Striker shuffles past me, flanked with the black shirt guards, who hold his elbows for safety and guidance. He walks down the row, weeping. I pull my cover completely over myself and clutch my book.

"Safe striding," someone calls.

"Hail Odin," says another.

Then another long silence, and from the other cell next to mine comes York's soft, penetrating voice. "I'm next, you bastard. I'm next."

After Striker is killed, his body is unhooked from the medical vine. The corpse valets quickly strip off his soiled uniform, which will be laundered and sent on to the next inmate, and tumble his naked corpse on one of the battered metal cafeteria carts. An old paint-spattered throw cloth is tossed over the corpse. The valets wait until the area is cleared of all the witnesses before they wheel Striker's carcass to the crematorium.

When they built this enchanted place, the idea was to make it self-sufficient. They started farms outside the prison walls that were once plowed by the short-timers. Those fields lie fallow now, taken over by wild mustard. They built grinders for the wheat that was grown, and giant mixing bowls for the bread to feed the men—coarse bread with the hulls of the wheat still inside. Those bowls now lie turned on their sides in forgotten basement rooms, filled with dust, and the grinders were dismantled and taken away years ago to be sold as scrap metal. They built factories so the inmates could make their own clothes out of wool that was at that time carded at the women's prison. The factory is still housed in Building G, but now the convicts make a popular brand of clothing called Convict Blues that is sold for outrageous prices on the outside. They built an infirmary and a tiny chapel in the yard. That chapel is now the rape shed.

The idea a century ago was that the men lived here until they died, and as they lived, they should be no burden to others. When they died, their ashes were to die here, too. There was no reason to waste money on paupers' graves. How much easier, the first warden thought, if we just burned the dead.

And so a crematorium was built. There are almost three thousand inmates in this prison, with the number being constantly replenished. Men die here all the time, of age and of each other, and so smoke often rises from the graying, sooty smokestack behind Cellblock H.

The oven is buried deep in the basement, in a catacomb of boilers. The oven is nondescript. It could be a big bread oven. It has a metal door with a coiled heavy latch. The inside is scarred with the heat flashes of metal fillings and metal body parts burning.

It is very late when Striker is wheeled across the yard. The moon glows on the dusty dirt. The valets take the creaking elevator down into the basement with the body and leave it at the oven door. Striker's white legs dangle out from under the haphazard drop cloth. He joins two other bodies on carts. One is Daniel Trubock, the famous wife killer, dead of a gunshot that has been classified a head injury. The other is a nameless old man. He came here years ago on a minor charge—shoplifting—and ended up spending decades of his life in one of the metal coffins of Cellblock H, singing like a loon.

Two new guards come down the metal steps, pulling on thick heat-proof gloves. They open the metal oven door.

Taking hands and feet, the guards load the inmates in the oven. Naked except for a swatch of dark pubic hair and a set of faded navy tattoos on flaccid arms, Striker is tumbled into the oven. His white buttocks look like two narrow white stones.

The door is slammed shut, and the dial for the fire is turned on. The oven heats to 1800 degrees, but it is old and cranky. It takes between three and five hours to burn the bodies, depending on how many men are inside.

No one likes to be by the oven when the men burn, not even the female guards, who seem the toughest and most able to take death. The burning bodies make hissing and popping sounds. When the heads explode from the trapped steam, they make a particularly gruesome sound, like giant bugs being thwapped.

The guards leave and go up the narrow metal stairs to a small damp lunchroom. They eat their packed lunches and drink weak coffee from Styrofoam cups. Neither has much of an appetite. The male guard reads a car magazine. His female counterpart knits a pair of blue baby socks for her best friend's baby.

"Did you ever expect to be working here?" the male guard asks her at one point.

The woman shakes her head, eyes on the dangling bootie. "But in this economy, I'm not complaining." She has a friendly working-class smile.

"I'll just be glad when probation is up and we can get away from the oven," he says.

All new guards spend their probation at the oven. If you can handle the despair of the oven, you can handle anything. And it is a good place, away from the inmates, for the guards to learn the unspoken rules of the prison. There is one set of rules they teach the guards on paper, but it is the unwritten rules that matter.

It is almost dawn when the guards head back down the steps. They open the smoking door and stand back, waving away the cloying smoke.

"This job has ruined barbecue for me," the male guard jokes.

The female guard immediately responds, "Now you made me want pork ribs!"

The male guard shakes his head, laughing at her.

They shovel out the hot ashes into coffee-can urns stacked on another old cafeteria cart. They rush and scrape the ashes into the cans. The ashes of the dead men get all mixed up, and who is to complain? When the cans are full, the male guard hammers down the metal lids, and the woman writes the inmate numbers on the top with a black marker. There are no names on the urns. You die a number here.

When they are done, the female guard rakes the oven for any fillings or metal pins while the male guard wheels the new cans into one of the rooms that line the basement like so many closets for the dead.

Wall after wall of ashes are stored on tall wooden shelves in these rooms. Years of flooding have rotted the shelves and rusted the cans. In some rooms, the shelves have fallen and gigantic clumps of cans are fused together with rust into shapes like strange metal gargoyles. In summers, the wet cans dry out and then slowly bulge and explode. Rivers of gray ash have run down the shelves, leaving drifts of ashes on the floor. Over time, an inch of compacted ashes has accumulated on the basement floors. It seeps and sifts down through the broken concrete, so if you dug ten feet or more under this basement, you would find soil riddled with currents of ash.

The male guard walks through this coating as he finds a space and tosses the three new cans on a heap of others on a top shelf. The dried ashes make a gritty sound and stick to the treads of his black work boots.

When the guards are done, they turn off the dim lights and leave the basement. A nugget of a tooth has gotten stuck in the treads of the male guard's boots, and he stops on the metal stairs on the way up to gouge it out with his regulation knife. The female guard waits patiently for him, one hand resting on the railing.

The oven ticks as it cools down. The last of the sweet-smelling smoke rises from the chimney.

That is when the flibber-gibbets come out.

I am afraid to talk about the flibber-gibbets. Out of all the wonderful, beautiful, and enchanted things in this place, the flibber-gibbets scare me more than anything else.

They come out into the oven room, small and gray, holding their swollen little cannibal bellies with their hands, groaning with pain as if about to give birth. I can smell them even from where I am—they smell like cinnamon sugar gone bad. The flibber-gibbets do not scramble and snicker like the little men with their hammers. They do not sigh and slap like Risk and his cronies. They do not fight like York or cry in pain like the white-haired boy or enjoy the cool grip of the phone like Conroy. They do not lie like the lady or freeze like the priest or try so hard like the warden.

They do nothing that is human, and this is what frightens me.

The flibber-gibbets writhe on the warm floor in front of the oven, gripping their swollen bellies. I can picture the slippery gray coils of death inside them, just waiting to be squeezed into promise.

Their macabre dance over, the flibber-gibbets slowly rise. They go room to room, sniffing for the new cans. They climb up the shelves with silent determination, gripping the rotted wood with their razor-sharp teeth. They make no sound as they find the new cans, still warm with the ashes. They crawl over the cans, their eyes narrowing as they bend arms and legs like insects or reptiles seeking warmth. They bite one another with bland fury if one gets in the way. Their bite marks leave open gray wounds like dead clay. No blood or fluid comes from the wounds. You could put a penny in each gray slot.

When I am dead, I will be put in the oven and burned and shoveled into a can like Striker and the others. I am okay with that. I will be no more than ashes. It would be better if I were less, but a can of ashes is okay.

What I don't like is the thought of the flibber-gibbets climbing over my new warm metal skin. I don't like to think of myself wrapped in their limbs, taking the last of my kindling warmth.

But I know that this enchanted place comes with its own vision. My eyes are not the eyes of the Lord. My eyes are not the eyes of the lizards among us, of the dirt and the stones and the bloody hearts. This is the way it is. That is the way it should be.

The day after Striker's execution, the light above me flickers to tell me the news—the golden horses are going to run. They always seem to run around the time of an execution. I can see their gold-flecked nostrils and bronzed skin, their hard flexing muscles and wild dark eyes. Their eyes are like dark agates or like the color of bronze poured to iron—eyes like the lady's. Or York's. Dark eyes that see nothing as they run but the pure wild joy in movement.

It is brassy daylight out, and the men of the yard stop and feel the horses' movements under their feet. Risk and his cronies at the weight pile stop and feel the trembling under their feet. The whole enchanted place stops and tilts its head to listen.

Go, horses! I think. Go. And they do, running with magic and stretching desire, their flanks out and their tails a whiplash of gold, their manes streaming nothing but butter yellow. No one rides them; no one could. They stretch their bodies underground as if the sun lived there and could rise and warm the earth above, warm it like molten metal. I hear the pounding even from my dungeon, see the faint powder erupt on the walls as they go thundering past. Go, horses! I think. Go.

Another loop and the tremors come again. Another pass and the beating of hooves as they pound past my cell wall. The men on the yard sway, uncertain, and there is a holler from a guard tower. "All down," the fool yells. Doesn't he know the horses are running? The men drop for fear of a rifle shot to the back of the skull, and it is for the best, because as they fall, they lie on the ground and feel the clods under their hands. They can feel the golden horses moving, feel their muscles, and feel their strength as they pass.

A voice pipes in from a bandstand far away. It sounds like an old-fashioned radio voice. Nine, it says, eight or six. Four, maybe. The horses run with names no one can understand. Richard, Glenn, Plato. Men try to name them, but men cannot name anything as wild and unpredictable as these horses. Who could name such power? They defy names. One more time, please, I pray, and my prayer is rewarded as the trembling begins, and the horses are suddenly right on the other side of my wall, running so close to the stone that freshets of dust and mica shake from the walls to rain like silver dust on my floor. I fall to the floor and sift their precious dust and I can see them, their hard metal bodies, the way the gold rises to cream on their backs and flows off in ripples of heat, how their eyes are wide with pleasure and their nostrils flared, the smoke of desire bellowing from them.

Go, horses! Run! The whole dungeon is trembling with the heat of their pass, and I can hear the other men of the row cry out with something like fear and wonder as our walls shake. Their hooves are retreating once more, and I am on my knees, my hands swaying in unspeakable pleasure in the fresh dust they have shed.

The radio calls from farther away. The tower lights flash and then flash again, and the men rise from the dirt of the yard outside, dusting it off from their hands, laughing embarrassedly to each other. They do not stop to listen carefully for the sound of the golden horses as they retreat far underground. They do not feel the pang I do at knowing the horses ran so close to me and have ridden away once again.

I do not know when they will come back. They have cleaved back down to the underworld, where red rivers burn and cliffs ignite. I do not know the name of the place they come from. It could be hell or heaven or the gate to either—it defies me as much as their names. But I know the golden horses gallop there, their manes like tongues of fire, their legs stretched out with the pure joy of running, their hooves unafraid of damning the dirt.

The lady is not at the prison during Striker's execution. She is never around during the executions, not of her clients, not of others. She feels for the priest that he has to be there, but watching men die holds little interest for her.

She is more interested in the living.

She takes the photo of little York and his mother back to Auntie Beth, as promised. The thrill of the blue forest does not abate for her. She hopes to stay the night in the same motel, hopes to spy rental signs for cabins along the way—just dreaming, she tells herself.

Auntie Beth is quiet on this visit. The lady is accustomed to that. A fatigue sets in with the families she works with. There comes a point when all the secrets are told and all that is left are their spent ghosts. She has told Auntie Beth that once the case is over, she will disappear from her life. She always tells the families this important truth.

So they enjoy their friendship for the moment, wrapped in the early-afternoon glow on the front porch as they sit together.

Auntie Beth rubs at her swollen toes, wrapped

in her huge pilled slippers. "He gonna die?" she finally asks.

"I don't know," the lady softly answers. "Sometimes they do."

Auntie Beth nods, sighs. She looks at the hills. No promises. The lady sees that she has rubbed a little lipstick for rouge on her cheeks, tidied her iron hair with old clips. These little efforts by families for her visits always touch the lady to the quick.

"Gonna cry when it happens, even if he deserves it."

"Of course."

"You know where his mama is buried?"

"No."

"I'll get you the address." The old woman hesitates and then busks her knees against the lady: a quick gesture but a knowing one. "I want to ask you. . ." she stops.

"Yes?"

"I was gonna ask—those poor girls." Auntie Beth stops. Her chin trembles, and the lady sees grief even in her teeth.

"Yes," the lady says. Her voice sounds like it can absorb a river of tears.

"You'll say sorry for me? To their families?"

"Yes," the lady says. "I will tell them sorry from you."

The old woman breaks down in tears, there on her front porch, and eventually, the lady reaches one hand over and holds her shoulder as she sobs.

The lady feels drained as she makes it to the address Auntie Beth has given her. It isn't much as far as addresses go, but it's easy to find: the back grounds of the state mental hospital.

They used to have paupers' graves back then. She thinks of the crematorium at the prison and wonders which is worse: to be buried a number or burned?

The slot for York's mom seems too narrow for a body, and the lady has a gruesome image of the pauper corpses laid side by side, endlessly spooning under the earth. York's mother was one of these, entombed in a shroud, buried with dirt thrown over her and only the sky watching. No one was here to say goodbye. There is just a small rusted metal nameplate lined up with the others. There is a date of her death but no date of her birth. Perhaps they didn't care to check.

The lady looks up and sees she is standing among hundreds of nameplates, stretching to the desultory woods behind the old hospital grounds. The newer grounds—the fancy places they parade for the public—are up front, fresh with splashed pastel paint and sculptures and a big fancy building.

But the truth is back here, the lady thinks, buried in a slot too narrow to contain a body. York's mother. Shirley. Buried like thousands of other mentally disabled people over the years, nameless and willed to be forgotten.

She reminds herself to make sure her mother has a proper grave when she passes, with a headstone and her name and nice flowers at the side. The normal people in the graveyard can scoot over a bit, she thinks, and make way for Mom. The thought makes her smile.

The lady is glad that she came. Sometimes the roads she takes don't bring her anyplace she can offer in court, but they give her insight all the same. It feels good to stand with her beaten black boots crunching the dirt above York's mother's bones, to feel a recognition: You existed, you counted, you were here.

She takes a picture of the grave, because you never know. Maybe York would like to see where his mom is buried.

As she leaves, she passes an old pink building with windows weeping rust, surrounded by a falling cyclone fence. She looks to the iron bars of the windows and remembers this was once the chil-

dren's ward, where, for infamous decades, children
as young as eight were housed in nightmarish con-
ditions, drugged with heavy psychotropic medica-
tions, and, she has heard, raped by older kids. She
has heard stories of what life was like for the children in that building, before they shut it down.

And then she goes looking for the doctors who
treated York's mother before she died.

Unknown days have passed. I am sitting on my cot,
thinking about dust. The dust from the horses running after Striker's execution settled over my cell. I
have taken care to disturb it as little as possible. I
like how it looks, mantled over the stone.

Slowly, my footprints mar the floor. I can't help
it. I have to get up to use the toilet, to take the food
trays.

The footprints look like reptile prints—like
a prehistoric monster has been walking my floor,
striding with mincing feet toward my cot.

I crouch on my cot and hold the blanket over me.
I pretend the monster is coming for me. Is he coming? Is he not?

There are some things I can never discuss. One is
the bad thing I did after I was released from the
mental hospital when I was eighteen. I wouldn't

want the idea of this thing to be in the world. Ideas are powerful things; we should take more care with them. I know there are some who would disagree— those who think ideas are like food they can taste and then spit out if they don't like it. But ideas are stronger than that. You can get a taste of an idea inside you, and the next thing you know, it won't leave. Until you do something about it.

As soulless as I am, I do not want others to do what I have done. Some ideas need to stay silent inside me, like the letters inside some words.

I am not afraid to tell about the second bad thing, the one that got me sent from general population to this dungeon. I can tell it because I know what I did and why I did it. You can read about it in the court trial transcripts.

"Warden, what did you find the day of March fourth?"

"I found a body at the bottom of stairwell 4A."

"Tell me about that stairwell."

"It serves the library."

"Okay. Tell me more."

"I was called at 0900."

"Please elaborate."

"A trusty had found a body."

"Warden. Please be more forthcoming."

"The body was of an inmate. Number 114657."

"And?"

"He had been bludgeoned about the head—no, that is not accurate. His head had been crushed against the steps."

"And what was the cause of death?"

"Profound brain injury."

I can see the spots even now.

"Warden, tell me. Did you eventually identify a suspect?"

"Yes."

"And how?"

"The suspect was sitting next to the corpse—crying."

"Please point him out to the court."

The warden points to me.

"Crying, you say."

"Yes. Well, weeping. Silently."

"What did he say?"

"Nothing at that time. He doesn't talk."

"Doesn't talk because he can't or doesn't talk because he won't?"

Here the court record shows a long pause.

"I can't say."

"Warden, that's not correct, and you know it. I understand there is a time on the record when the defendant is known to have spoken. There is, in fact, a recording."

"Yes. To my knowledge."

"So he can talk."

"Sir, it is not up to me to judge what someone can do."

I remember how the warden found me there, crying on the stairs, absently wiping blood all over my face as I wept. The warden had looked down with a sad expression and slowly pulled his service pistol from the holster. I could tell what he was thinking: It was him and me alone on the stairs and no one to say what went down.

"Okay. Fine. But your investigation determined he was the culprit."

"Yes. From the blood and brain matter on his hands."

"In other words, he was red-handed."

My attorney calls out with a tired voice: "Objection."

This time there were no high-powered attorneys or crowds in the courtroom. There was no fizzle or pop of cameras. No newspaper covered the story; one prison inmate killing another is not newsworthy. There was no one like the lady to explain how I was supposedly a product of my past. There was just me, my court-appointed attorney, the district attorney, the judge, and a group of tired jurors in the prison courtroom who wanted to go home.

The only mystery for them was why I had done it. Had he said something to me? Raped or hurt me? No one knew. There were just the two of us, and one was dead, and one of us would not speak.

Only the warden knew.

I wanted to ask him later, Why didn't you shoot me, warden? You could have raised your service pistol and ended me with a spray of blood and bone. I lifted my head for you—you could see I wasn't going to fight it. You could have filed a report that said self-defense. You didn't even need to file a report. You could have just tumbled me off to the oven and been done with me. No one would have cared. Many would say it would have been a blessing not just for me but the family of my victim.

The warden had just looked down at the dead man next to me, at his bashed head and leaking soft wet brains over the stone steps. He saw the inmate number on the prison shirt. He recognized the heavy face and narrow rabbit teeth. He knew this inmate from the library, watching that day. He knew who the inmate was and what kind of man he was—a man like Risk.

The warden knew what my life was like outside the library. The question for him was not why I had killed this man. It was why I had waited so long.

Even if the outside saw another nameless number, even if the mattresses of my life said just another, the warden saw something different. He saw what had been done to me. He saw *me*. And in that moment, I mattered. He holstered his pistol and he reached down and he took my bloody hand. He raised me up. He said he would take me someplace safe, someplace no one would ever hurt me again.

My attorney tried to point out that I had been good for many years—a model inmate, he said, spending all his time in the library. Even that didn't matter when they found me sitting next to another nameless number, crying with his brains on my hands.

That is the way murder is. It isn't like TV. It isn't like the books. It is holding a man's head in your hands as his eyes flutter and die. It is watching the blood pour and the body twitch and thinking how easy it was. It is thinking: At least it is better this time, I made it quick. And: At least I didn't look inside.

The warden was the last one called to testify. No mitigation, no worries. There was no jury weeping this time, no woman moaning in the back row, and it was for the better.

The warden passed me on his way off the stand. I didn't look up at him. I was hiding behind my hands the entire trial, having been shaved of my hair by the prison doctors. But I felt the warden when he passed, and I knew the gift he had given me. It was the gift of privacy.

It took only an hour this time for the jury to decide. Death.

I was glad when the warden led me to the dungeon. I was glad when he opened this cell door himself and I stepped inside, knowing I would never leave again until the last journey. By that time I had realized others could see the monsters coiled under my skin, see the screaming fear. They could see the wet mattresses and splayed legs and all that has come before and could come again.

I couldn't have that. Not anymore.

I knew that I would never again see the beautiful soft-tufted night birds outside the window, never again sit in the library with the slanting sun through the bars. And that was okay, because I brought those ideas with me, stored in my heart.

Even in the dungeon, I cover my head with my blanket. Whether heaven or whether hell, I will never escape who I am. The only answer now is to wait. We are all safer that way, just as the warden knows.

Since I came to the dungeon, time has lost all meaning. I cannot tell you exactly how long I have been down here. The lightbulb in the metal cage above me flickers on at what I think is morning, and it turns off at what I guess is night, but unless I were to mark the walls, I have no way of knowing how many years have passed. I could tell you about the books I have read, and I could tell you of the times when the horses have run—with every execution, it seems—and of the random times when the little men come to visit, and of the dark times when these halls fill with pain. But I cannot tell you of time.

If I could talk, I could ask others, "What year is it? What day? What number?" But what would be the point of that? What would that number tell me?

Anyway, time is more than counting days. On the outside, people think clocks tell them the time. They set an alarm for work and wake up to a blinking light that says six a.m. They look to an office wall to tell them if it is time to go home. The truth is, clocks don't tell time. Time is measured in meaning. *I better get up for work* or *It's time to feed the baby*. Or *That was the year I got cancer* or *That is the day we celebrate your birthday*. Or *Remember when our father died* or *Let's remember to plant turnips this spring*. It is meaning that drives most people forward into time, and it is meaning that reminds them of the past, so they know where they are in the universe.

What about for men like me? For us, time doesn't exist. The measurements of life—birth, death, loss, marriage, love, lust, happiness—have no meaning in this dungeon. Time passes here, but it doesn't count. I could have a clock, but what would the dial tell me? Nothing.

When time no longer exists, you don't care about getting up, you don't think about birthdays, you don't think back to people you lost. You float free in the universe, untethered to anyone or anything. Your heart is empty, and because your heart is empty, you have no time. You have no place in the universe.

At least I used to think this way. Only listening to the lady and the priest has made me feel a little different.

I think more about time now. Not for me but for the lady.

Time is running out for the lady, and she doesn't even know it. I hear the pain in her walk, and I feel it float in tendrils through my bars. The lady is searching for time. She is searching for a way to tether herself to someone. Deep in her secret heart, in the pure place she protects, she is afraid she will always be alone—that she will go through life without being known. And she will not survive that.

The lady is afraid she will wake up one morning

and learn the answer she asked herself about York: When do you know you want to die?

I wish I could talk to her. I would tell her, "Lady, it is not a slow awakening. And it is not a sudden revelation. No, it is when you wake up and realize you no longer have time."

For the first time in my life, I want to help someone. I want the lady to find what I cannot know—the gift of time.

The lady and the priest are sitting on a picnic bench by the old rectory building right outside the prison. The old rectory house is faded white. The windows are shuttered with plywood. At one time the prison priest lived here. Now the prison uses it for storage, since the priest has a small apartment in the nearby town, a place with a little kitchen and a backyard and a battered gas stove.

The priest has imagined many times what it would be like to invite the lady over for dinner. He likes to cook. It is one of his few pleasures. He has not gotten up the courage to ask her. He thinks ruefully that he doesn't know how to ask a lady out—he has never done it.

The lady has brought her lunch, and he has joined her. The lady eats a container of cold pasta salad from a nearby deli. She sees the food he has brought—homemade vegetable soup in a thermos, rich and fragrant with chunks of zucchini, the broth floating with herbs—and she is embarrassed by her sanitized lunch.

They are silent for a time, and the lady pushes around her cold salad. She puts down the plastic fork and opens a package of crackers. "Why did you leave the priesthood?" she asks.

He takes a deep breath of relief. He has been waiting for this question.

"I was resentful in my heart," he says immediately.

Her face invites the story.

"After eight years of education and four years in discernment, I had no idea what I really wanted or how I had gotten there." He tells her he felt a failure already, a promising boy from a respected church family. But there was something in him that was off-putting, a lack of confidence that his superiors warned him about more than once. "It's not that you lack humility," an instructor at the seminary had told him. "It's that you lack insight."

"When I was ordained, I got the rewards of their lack of confidence," he says. He was assigned to a dying Catholic church on the outskirts of the city. There would be no exciting work overseas for him, no dynamic action. His church had only a handful of parishioners left, almost all over the age of sixty.

"I pretended to myself that I wanted to make our little church into a force. Now I know I was only cherishing the resentment in my heart."

The lady listens. A damp breeze off the river has picked up, the summer day unnaturally cool. The priest sees her shiver a bit in her cardigan. He pours the fragrant vegetable soup from the thermos into the cup and pushes it to her. "The church ladies suggested bingo nights and Christmas raffles and spaghetti suppers and missions to the city soup kitchen to feed the poor on Thanksgiving. I went along with all of it, but to tell the truth, I didn't know why I was really there."

"Who does?" The lady gently smiles, drinking the soup.

"If the devil waits for an open door, I had the whole house open, and it was catching a breeze," he says, his eyes faraway as he opens a bag containing two homemade rolls. He butters one for her. "But it was not the devil that made me do it."

He tells her it started when a fellow priest from a much larger, popular church reached out to him, inviting his congregation to join their effort to combat child sex trafficking. He would never forget the innocent and appalling words of one trembling church parishioner on their first night of doing outreach. "But where are the red lights?" the woman had asked.

The kids on the corners didn't look victimized. They looked hard. And they were as repelled by his church ladies as they were by any zealot with a fistful of guilt and silver coins of regret. A child prostitute in his church, he had to admit, would live a life of cloying stigma. He saw the choices they were being offered through their eyes—momentary charity with a bounty of shame or prideful indifference.

That first night, the group walked the cold winter streets, handing out brochures for local programs. The next night, half as many of his devoted followers showed up, and the night after that, he was the only one to go. He understood the cold was too much, the streets too hard. It was easier to plan the winter raffle and the Thanksgiving soup kitchen trip.

That night he ended up walking those night streets alone, a warm jacket over his collar and clerical shirt.

Why did he go into the club? He didn't know. He told himself he wanted to help. But he was confused. His entire life had been spent following his anointed path, like Hansel and Gretel following their trail of crumbs, and instead of finding happy ever after, he found a house built of candy and a hot oven of confusion.

The club was neat and clean. There was a faint smell of bleach. Some of the tables had solitary men sitting at them. A small stage was frocked with silver tinsel. A girl was on it. It took him a moment to realize she was naked. In this setting, her nakedness looked almost ordinary. He had always been chaste, but he was not innocent. The entire scene was devoid of sensuality. He felt as safe as in a library.

A server put down a napkin. Five dollars for a soda drink? Apparently, yes.

He sat for a while, feeling strangely relaxed. He had no idea what he was doing, but he was here. He sipped his soda.

Songs played. Girls rotated slowly throughout the room. One came over to his table. She was young and fresh-looking, with round cheeks and puppy fat on the sides of her waist.

"Want a table dance?" she asked.

He shook his head, not knowing what that was.

"Buy me a drink?"

"Sure."

She sat down, and immediately, the server was there. The girl ordered a large Diet Coke, and the priest was out ten dollars and could see the deal.

"How old are you?" he asked, looking at her bright skin.

"Sixteen." She shrugged, sipping the soda. Seeing the alarm in his face, she quickly added, "But I have a license that says I'm of age. You aren't a cop, are you?" She looked with innocence at his Roman collar.

"I'm a priest," he told her, and felt thankful when she didn't make the obligatory child molester joke.

She drank her soda and told him her story. How she had been living on the streets since she was fourteen, and how lucky she was to work in this club because it was a safe, good place and she made money and had her own apartment. She had plans—she was getting her GED. "I'm going to go to community college," she boasted. How her most favorite book of all was *Watership Down*. Her story had the artlessness of truth, and in the end, it all turned out to be true. She was exactly who she said she was.

"I'm wasting time," she said with a laugh after they had been chatting for a little while.

"How so?" he asked.

"Sitting here and not dancing," she said, and he looked around and saw what she meant. "Do you want a table dance?" she asked hopefully. "Ten dollars for one song."

"No, thanks." He smiled. He got up to go.

"I'm hungry," she said, and before he knew it, he was going to get some food from the jazz club across the street. Her pasta dish cost more than he'd paid for food over a day, but he bought it. He returned with the Styrofoam container and watched her eat. She didn't offer to pay him back.

They became friends. There was no better way to put it. He was sure in his heart that he was not going back in order to do her harm.

The night came when he was in the club as her shift was ending. He offered her a ride. For the first time, he saw the fear and vulnerability in her eyes. With a start, he realized that she had been one of those hard kids on the corner. He could see her tabulate the odds of accepting his ride, not just physically but emotionally.

"Okay," she said in an unsure voice.

She rode silently in his car for a while, her hand on the handle. Finally, like the teenager she was, she could no longer maintain silence and broke into conversation, telling him all sorts of stuff about her little sister, a girl named Stephanie who lived in foster care. "She likes seafood," she burbled. "I'm going to buy her a leather jacket for Christmas."

Her apartment was a studio in a run-down building above the freeway. His heart vanished

when he heard the cockroaches scatter as she turned
on the light, and he saw the downturned shame in
her soft, round face. Why had he thought it would be
better? She was a teenager fresh off the streets.

"It's clean," he offered.

There was a bed made with one blanket and
a flat pillow. A tiny kitchen had a saucepan in the
strainer on a cracked linoleum counter. There was
an opened box of Cheerios on the upper shelf and
a stack of three tuna cans. "I like tuna," she explained. There was an impossibly tiny refrigerator
that he discovered later had exactly enough room
for a pint of milk, a small jar of mayo, and one container of take-out Chinese. A single shelf held three
mismatched coffee cups, two with broken handles.
The main room had built-in shelves that stood for
dressers and, incongruously, a bright pink plastic
beanbag chair. "A friend gave me that," she said of
the beanbag chair.

She dropped on the floor the duffel bag that contained her dancing clothes and ridiculous plastic
wedge high heels. He said good night, and he tried
not to think why she looked sad when he left.

On the way down, he got stuck in the old rickety
elevator with the folding accordion doors and had
to be rescued by an old woman with black starling
eyes who told him all about the pet clinic next door

and how they performed experiments on the animals they stole.

The hot tea he drank after meals now tasted like mud. The shower in the morning after a long run felt like a waste of water, the run a waste of time. His sermons—his one source of pride, because he had such a strong voice—now felt like artifice. One night he put down his Bible and looked out the window blinds of his rectory apartment and thought about the layers of life a man can live without even knowing his shadow lives on the floors below.

He hungered to see her. It was not a sexual hunger or a romantic hunger. He just wanted to see her.

He knew she was using him in the way that she used everyone. He knew it wasn't personal; that was how she had learned to get by. She delighted in getting him to pay for things, yelling, "Score!" when he did, and he would turn to look at her, so happy to have a thrift store book or a cheap pair of tights, and feel a welter of emotions inside.

Little by little she told him her past, but when she saw it diminished her in his eyes, she stopped. Instead, she became the brassy jokester, the laughing one. He liked her best when he took her places he thought she had never been, like the Japanese gardens or the zoo. Only later would she fess up that other men, at other times, had taken her to those places. For a girl of sixteen, she had a surprising breadth of experience, from living in a commune with her parents as a child to hitchhiking down the coast by herself. He thought of what he was doing as a child—hiding in his bedroom, reading the Bible, and fantasizing about being the pope—and felt embarrassed.

She hated her parents. "Fucking hippies," she said with scorn. "Communes of destruction." She kept a comic pinned to her wall that showed an angry hippie threatening to bust out of his commune because of the crabs, and she laughed every time she looked at it. He had to ask her what it meant by crabs and was repelled at her artless description.

He tried to reason with her about her work, if you could call it work. "I'm the one in power," she argued almost belligerently. "They're the ones who sit there and give me the money."

She talked about her future as if people could reinvent themselves like snakes shedding their skins. "It may not be so easy," he said, but she just looked at him like he was the one who didn't know anything.

There were things she never discussed. There were strange scars on her palms, like slashes. It wasn't until much later, when he took the job at the prison, that he realized these were scars from defensive wounds. She had a soiled white rabbit's foot she carried with her everywhere, and a creased picture of a blond girl she said was her best friend on the streets who went missing during the time when a notorious serial killer was active.

She confused him. Who was she? Who was this laughing child, this woman, this victim of abuse, this well-read teenager, this dancer?

"How come I can't be all of them?" she asked him plaintively when they had driven all night through the silk black skies above an old country road, just driving and driving, and he voiced this thought out loud. "Why can't I be all?"

That's what he thought of later, but he also thought about those little moments—the cans of tuna, the pink plastic beanbag chair, her hips under the club lights, the turned-away eyes, and most of all, her awareness of those things in herself—that made him realize she was the first person who truly existed for him.

And so he fell in love for the first time. Not with her, necessarily; he fell in love with life.

The minute they did it—her mounting him in, of all places, the pink plastic beanbag chair—he saw her pull away from him like water going down a drain.

She had pushed it in so many ways, coming on to him. The more time they spent together—the more he really came to *know* her—the more she upped the sexual ante, flirting, rubbing herself on him, and joking and teasing, combing his hair with her fingers at the back of his neck. And then the minute she got it, her eyes went dark and distant and she was gone.

He tried to hold her in bed afterward, unsure how to reach her. He was in numb shock for what he had just done. He wanted comfort. She curled backward against him, the shock of her naked body pouring warmth down his stomach, but he felt she was a million miles away, lost in another place.

Later, he woke up to find her reading. She was back in the pink beanbag chair, wearing only a pair of old men's paisley boxer shorts, her worn copy of *Watership Down* cradled in one hand, the glasses she refused to let anyone see—huge pink insurance frames, the cheapest the eye doctor could provide—on her face. Her soft hair was gathered in a knot on top of her head. And her thumb was in her mouth.

She sucks her thumb, he thought. He closed his eyes before she could catch him seeing her like that, so naked, and for a long time his heart pounded in his chest like he had done something wrong.

The cool wind has picked up and shakes the leaves of the walnut and elm trees. The lady has wrapped her cardigan around her. The soup is gone, and the rolls are crumbs.

"What happened to her?" the lady asks.

He cannot tell her this—he does not want to tell her this.

"It lasted for months," he begins.

He could not face how much he meant to her and how much she tried to hide it. It was in the spaces between her writhing in bed and the searching, hopeless looks she gave him and the blankness when she stared at a full plate of food he had cooked for her. It was in his growing knowledge that she needed him and he was not able to accept her.

"And she knew," he says, his voice empty with grief.

"How did she know?"

"I told her I would not take her to my apartment."

He had been trying to explain that he couldn't take her to his rectory apartment, how unbelievably irrational it was for her to ask. He said it like he wasn't trying to escape a past himself. How they had two lives and both had meaning, how he was trying to wrestle with being a man of the cloth and a man who loved her.

"Trying to wrestle?" she had said acidly, her little-girl eyes gone cold. "Trying? When does the real action commence?"

He was shocked at her meanness. It was as if the venom of her life, the hatred of her past, all came out against him. The more he felt accused of failing her, the more the implacable resentment returned to his heart. Only now it wasn't just resentment against life. It was resentment against her.

As always, afterward, when they fought, she came to him and with urgency sought to wrap her legs around him. There was such a sad desperation in her lovemaking that he was repelled. "I *want* to love you," he whispered against her hard little chest, and he knew it sounded like a criticism—that the person she was could not be the person he needed to love. He felt her slip away in his arms to that cool, distant place, and this time he did not fight for her to come back.

He told himself he was taking a sabbatical. A much needed vacation. A respite.

No one in the church batted an eye. The truth was, they didn't care. Even blue-haired ladies know when they are despised.

He wimped out and told her at the last minute. He had taken her to dinner for her favorite meal, steak and potatoes and lots of bread and butter and salad. She still ate like she was a homeless kid, as if the calories might disappear at the next meal.

It wasn't until they were back at her place with

cockroaches fleeing under the light switch that he casually remarked he was leaving town for a few weeks.

"Where?" Her voice was shocked and bereft.

"Belize." It was just a vacation, he told himself.

She backed up across the floor, bewildered. In her face he could see the terror. He was just another man who had used her and exploited her and opened her legs and now was leaving, only he had done a hundred times worse: He had opened her heart.

"It doesn't have to be this way," he whispered.

She shook her head, and in that moment he saw the cheap pink beanbag chair and the dried Cheerios in the cereal bowl on the counter and he knew he was right to leave. It wasn't her poverty or her past. It was the shame she carried like a black cloud, a shame that reminded him of himself.

"I'll come back," he said, uncertain if it was true.

He says this to the lady, who still sits at the picnic table, wrapped in her cardigan. Her face is warm, her eyes on his face. He feels an immeasurable strength in her.

"You cannot ask what I did in Belize because I cannot remember. Did I read books? Cook? Eat? It doesn't matter. I was running away and knew it. When I got back to the airport after a whole month gone, I felt no better than when I left. Except I knew it was time to leave the priesthood." He pauses and takes a deep, shuddering breath. "My first call was to my superior. To let him know I was fallen and would be leaving, no questions to be asked. My second call was to her apartment. She was gone. The apartment was vacant. The landlord said she had just disappeared. I went to the club, and they said she had vanished. No one seemed to care. It was like she didn't matter, and I guess she didn't matter."

He is crying and doesn't realize it. The tears run down his cheeks.

The lady watches him cry. "She was *gone*," she says with finality.

"Yes. Gone. People go missing every day, but with her, it didn't matter. No missing persons reports. No parents to call the police, no one to even *notice.* I had never known how *alone* she was before, not really. But she was. She was completely alone except for me. And I left."

"Did she choose to say goodbye?" the lady asks.

He smiles a little at the kindness of this phrase. "If anyone ever wanted to say goodbye, she did. She jumped off a bridge. The police pulled her out a week later."

The lady tries to decide if she should touch him, while the silver tears flow down his cheeks. She reaches across the picnic table and picks up his cold hand. She holds it as though she is holding a cup.

He wipes his cheeks. For the first time, she sees a bloom in his pallid skin, as if he is coming back to life. The poison is leaving him.

"She was pregnant."

"Oh, you," the lady says, but the surprise for her is when he turns to let her see his face, she is crying, too.

The yard is so big, so full of bright pulsating colors—flowers so yellow they color your eyes, thick green grass that squeals between your teeth when you make it into a whistle, clotted racetrack dirt from one end to the other, and if you put your head down, you would surely hear them, the horses that run under that ground, all golden and lithe in the sunlight.

The men in the yard are hard and bright even on the darkest of days. They stand under the corrugated grandstand and look at the rainy sky, and oh, how that must feel. They see the giant drops gather on the metal poles, and they know if they licked the poles, they could taste the metal, and just by knowing that, they do taste it, and deep underneath them in my cell, I can taste it, too.

The yard smells when it rains in the summer.

It smells so strong that I can smell it way down in the depth of this dungeon. I can smell the dung from the golden horses rising through the dirt, and I think about each clod of mud and how it contains the history of the world: shards of mica and stone, glossy ribbons of clay too faint to see, the arm and leg of Eve, the pulsating pull of Adam. The taste of minerals can fling us out to sea and above to the skies. The world can be in one clod of dirt.

With every exhalation, I find a way out of this enchanted place. My breath rises to the clouds, and some tiny, microscopic particle joins with the clouds and condenses, and when it rains, that tiny part of me is returned to this earth—far away, maybe, in another place like China.

They can keep men in here, under lock and key, deep in the dungeon until the final moments of their lives, so that men like York and me will never taste the rain. But they cannot keep us from passing our condensation on to the sky. They cannot keep us from raining down in China.

The warden stands outside my cell. I peek at his face from under my blanket.

He looks sad. I wish I could say sorry about his wife having cancer. Unlike other men in the dungeon, I would mean it.

He is holding a letter stamped with large letters: LEGAL MAIL. This can mean only one thing. Someplace in the labyrinth of the legal system, my case has been flagged for appeal. I shake my head under the cover and turn my face to the wall.

"I know," the warden says soothingly. "But I have to give you your legal mail, and you have to sign that you read it."

I nod carefully under the cover.

He pushes the letter through the slot and steps respectfully away, turning his back. I scuttle forward to grab it and then hide under my blanket to read it.

The letter is from an attorney. He has been assigned to represent me through some defense fund. He wants to meet me, take on my case. He says he plans to hire the lady. They will get me out of here, get me back into general population. They will save my life. *We can get you off death row*, he writes. *You can live.*

If I write him back, he says, he will come. I will be chained in the Dugdemona cage. I will see the scrap of sky.

"Whatever you want," the warden says, his back still turned.

He drops the pencil stub through the slot. I scurry forward again and retreat to my cot with the pencil. I pick up the letter and sign that I read it. Then I write one word to the attorney: *No.*

I push the letter through the slot and wait back on my cot, my blanket over my head, until the warden retreats.

After he is gone, I realize I am still holding the pencil stub. I turn it over in my hands and taste the lead at its end.

The lady and the priest are sitting on one of the old wooden benches next to the stream that runs alongside the prison, where it widens into the pond. A century before, this is where they hanged people. The gallows are long gone, but marks from the wooden frame remain gouged into the soil. Still, it is a gracious place, cupped with trees, the tranquil water littered with the dust of summer. The lady has brought a bag of stale bread and is feeding a voracious group of mallards.

Was she sitting here, hoping the priest would see her as he left for the day? Yes. And he did, hope lighting his face when he saw her, walking faster than he knew.

They have been talking for over an hour as the sun begins to set, lighting the dust on the water, talking about her work and his and the men they both serve.

"You never talk about your family," the priest says to the lady.

Her heart stops. She looks into his face and sees only kindness. He has not said it out of malice or even curiosity. He is reaching for her, she can see.

She takes a breath and throws a crumb at the ducks. "My mother lives in a home. She has what people nowadays call intellectual disability."

"Oh." His face is calm but questioning.

"Mental retardation," she explains.

"Like York's mom."

She shoots him a glance. "Yes."

He holds his hand out for a bread crust. She puts it in his palm and feels the softness of touch.

"Is it hard, knowing?"

She shakes her head and then stops. "Maybe. I can understand."

He looks at her profile. There is something hidden in her face. "Your father?"

The question hangs there. "Which one?" she answers at last.

Something in her voice tells him. She expects he will recoil, but he doesn't. His face is full of tenderness. He looks at her for a long time. Her face is very still, her eyes on the pond.

"Another thing in common," he says softly.

She nods, a barely perceptible blink.

"It wasn't your fault."

She turns to him and lets him see right into her. Her eyes are luminous and bright and full of knowing.

"After a time," she says, "I liked it."

The lady watches the priest cross the parking lot and get into his battered older car. She wonders if she went too far but is too exhausted at the moment to care. I can accept your shame, she thinks. Can you accept mine?

The lady drives the long freeway back into the city. She thinks about her painful efforts at dating. The few attempts she made at telling men ended in disaster. She got wounded watching the disgust in their eyes, the recoil from her truth. She told herself this was the way it would be, that she was destined to live alone. Then came the priest and the warmth in her belly.

Even as she crests the hills from blackness into brightness, she knows a door in her heart has been opened. She wonders if she can will it closed again.

Back in her apartment, the lady sits at her desk, staring at a thick folder—memos, expert reports, old child welfare records, interviews she has done with others who lived in Sawmill Falls. There is even an interview with the psychiatrist who treated York's mom before she died in the mental hospital. There are birth certificates, death certificates, reports signed and notarized. Everything she needs for a new trial.

At the top is a lab test report where she has circled a finding in red ink. Twice.

She is done. She can feel it.

Her feelings can't tell her whether she will win. Sometimes she doesn't. Three times she has failed. And in those cases, she had found just as much or more evidence than she has for York. The decision is left to the judges. And a judge, she always reminds herself, is just a lawyer in a black robe.

Each time she failed, her client was executed. She waited each time to feel grief, but it never came. She felt sadness, and that was all. She knows too well how much pain these men caused others to feel true grief herself at their passing. The sadness she feels is more about a failed life.

She realizes she has kept the attorneys in the dark on this case. They do not know about Auntie Beth or Dr. Hammond or Troy Harney or the rabbit or the abuse, and they especially do not know that she ordered a blood test. They hired and paid her to tell them something, and all they have heard is nothing. For all they know, the last attorneys were right: There is nothing that can save York.

It wouldn't be hard to say she found nothing. There are some in her work who make a living doing as little as possible: investigators who work for attorneys like Grim and Reaper. There is no way of knowing the unknown—if she doesn't do her job, no one will know the difference.

She tells herself, You will do what you always do; you will take this folder to the attorneys. You will let them set the court date. You will let them argue your work in court as if they invented it themselves. You will sit in the shadows, unknown and unnamed in the papers, and when the news says your man walked off the row, you will nod and move on to the next case.

The calendar on the wall says July 22. She has time, if she acts soon.

Instead, she sits there. Her dark head bends forward, absorbed. She can see York, a little boy, running to his mom, seraphim limbs and a dark joyous smile. She can see his mother, daft but reaching for him. What would his mother think? she asks herself. And what of York? Born of one mistake, erased by others.

She thinks of her own mother. How often she heard that people like her mother should be sterilized. That it is better for people like her—and York—not to have been born than to be born and suffer.

She has a distinct memory of her mother sitting on their torn, buckled couch, trying to find a number in the phone book. "I keep trying," her mother would say, thumbing through the pages while chewing her lip. "Even if it takes a long time."

The lady feels a sharp pain. It is there, in her narrow chest. In the place we call a heart, in the place York wants to stop beating.

Lately, the warden has been coming to the row with his face pouched and the lower rims of his eyes red. He has the sourness of exhaustion on him, the glimmer of grief as he prepares for it to arrive.

He cleans up after his wife before he comes to work—the vomiting from the medicine, the hairs in the toilet bowl. He has fallen quiet with his wife, knowing that the quiet comforts her. He no longer brings up his day or asks about hers. She lies in their marriage bed, tubes at her side, and he can't help thinking how tubes end so many lives.

He still comes to work. He knows he could take time off, and there are men—Conroy in particular—who would eagerly take over. He also knows that his wife wouldn't like that. She wants to be alone in her pain. She is preparing to leave.

He hired hospice workers to come while he is at work. They change her bedding, wipe her face, empty and wash her bedpans. They are quiet with her, too. Margaret, the hospice workers call her, though he always called her his Madge, or Maggie. When they were young, she used to love being called Maggie—it sounded gay and Irish to her, as though she were a laughing lass. And she was, a bit. Now she is silent and waiting in a death row of her own making.

He wonders why so many easily accept death when it's caused by old age or cancer or even suicide, yet refuse to endorse death by execution. It seems wrong to him. No one deserves death more than someone like York or Striker or especially Arden. And yet those are the deaths that others will say are unnatural, not that of his dear sweet wife, a woman who raised three kids and never did anyone a wrong pass.

He knows when she passes, a grief will rip through him unlike anything he has ever known. Preparing for it doesn't help. He just knows it will come. It is like realizing you are sailing a boat across an ocean and soon you will find the other shore—it will be just you and acres of dry, blinding white sand. There may be trees on that island, and sun, and food, but none of it will feel or taste right, because you will stand there and realize: I am alone.

The lady comes down the stone stairs and hears the priest. He is in the cell of the inmate called Jeffries.

The priest is so absorbed in what he is doing he doesn't hear her approach. She stands outside the bars, watching. The priest is sitting beside Jeffries on the cot as if they are in an apartment and not a filthy, flea-ridden cell where the bed bugs crunch under each mattress.

The priest is reading a letter to Jeffries—a letter from his mother. Like most of the men on the row, she figures, Jeffries is illiterate. The priest reads the words slowly, letting Jeffries savor them, letting him nod as he goes.

Jeffries sits quietly next to the priest, his hands unchained. The guards don't care if the priest gets attacked; that is not their concern. Jeffries's eyes are large in his emaciated face. He looks like the photos you see of African children in starvation, wasted away to nothing in years of waiting.

The lady sees how confident the priest is in this moment—how relaxed he is, just reading a letter to a needful man. His shoulders are square, his face smiling. He stops to smile at Jeffries, and in looking at him, he sees her.

Their eyes connect, and she lets her breath go and smiles back.

The priest doesn't know the lady thinks about him all the time now. She thinks of him when she awakens, alone in her bed, the sun coming through the curtains. She thinks of him when she sees York in the cage. She thinks of him when she drives into the blue country and sees the cabins at the side of the road. She wouldn't want him to know she has looked up his address and even driven by his place, smoked with loneliness and yet warmth, one light burning in the window. She wonders what it would be like to knock on his door. To be welcomed inside, have her coat taken, feel his hands on her shoulders.

The lady doesn't know that the priest thinks of her, too. He dreams of one touch that turns into a thousand. He expects he will be afraid, and he is, but something bigger is being born inside him. He has been looking for a calling all his life, he thinks, when maybe the calling was simpler than he ever thought.

My food comes three times a day, pushed through the slot of my door. It comes on a tarnished metal tray that is scratched and dull with graffiti. The prison tried plastic trays for a time until they realized the inmates were breaking them apart to make shanks out of the shards. The metal is safer.

I look forward to the trays more than the food. The food has grown more and more awful over time. When I first came here, at least it was real food. Even if the meat was full of gristle and the bread stale, it was recognizable as food. Now it is hard to say what it is. Breakfast is usually a wet dish of powdered eggs sitting in a puddle of stale water that tastes like powdered soap. Lunch might be a pile of chopped old melons, slippery with rot, with a paper cup of watered-down Tang. Dinner is usually a slab of mystery meat, pink-gray and strangely soft. They used to call this meat loaf until an inmate sued and actually won: The jury tasted the strange conglomeration of ingredients and refused to call it meat.

Dinner often comes with a pile of gray-green stuff cooked to mush. It is hard to figure out what it is. The prison takes recalls and throwaways that even soup kitchens won't accept. When a store has a Dumpster of rotten squash or past-due meat or vegetable trimmings gone yellow with age, they go down the list of charities to call, from homeless shelters to African food agencies to church soup kitchens. It is only when none of these charities wants the food that they call the prisons. They unload the garbage for pennies a pound. There is even a huge black market of selling recalled food to prisons. Black-market criminals buy truckloads of recalled meat or peanut butter or other tainted foods, scrape them into new containers, and sell the stuff dirt-cheap to prisons. For months at a time, food poisoning sweeps our prison, and the oven is busy.

I get so hungry, I eat anyhow.

I get through it by watching the scratched tray appear under the disappearing food. Then I see the secret codes the inmates write to each other, like cave paintings. If the prison intelligence officers wanted to know about inmate communication, they would stop having the little men with hammers plant bugs in our cells, and read the trays instead.

An arrow pointing north. This means the Norteños.

Days later, another message comes underneath: a triangle, the signifier for a command table, and then a question mark.

Another question mark follows, and the answer comes again. This time there is a sound around the prison, like the bracing of steel inside the walls.

A crude drawing of a duck with a circle around it.

This means downing a duck. A duck is a guard.

A sharp intake of breath so hard that the dust rises from our walls.

Is there a taker?

The Aryans respond first with a circle and a slash. They are out. Too hot.

A few meals later, comes an answer. The Norteños will take care of it. They owe someone a favor.

It is a business that will require silence from everyone inside these walls, a business so important that the walls cannot talk.

A guard needs to die.

The female guard who knits booties for her friend's baby walks the yard to the oven. It will be a night like any other—she is thinking she will be glad when her probation is over and she can take a regular shift away from the oven. Despite the black humor and horror of working the oven, she likes this place. She likes moving among men who do not see her as a woman despite being deprived of women for so long. She likes being respected.

She thinks about an odd conversation she had recently with the intelligence officer Conroy. She'd heard information that the leader of the Norteños was dealing drugs through a corrupt guard in the visiting room. Following procedure, she promptly reported it to Conroy. "I took the precaution of putting the inmate into administrative segregation," she had said, her back rigid as she reported. She was proud of her deportment. She sounded almost like a cop instead of what she was, a single mom whose last job was at a Ross Dress for Less.

Conroy had seemed surprised—surprised and then pleased. He lavishly complimented her diligence. He asked her if she had made a report and seemed impressed that she had. "Is this the only copy?" he asked, taking it, and without thinking, she had said yes. And then as she was leaving, she turned to see his measured blue eyes on her, his hand on the phone.

The entire conversation felt wrong, she thinks. She wonders what has happened with the investigation. She will ask the warden about it.

A man darts from the shadows of Cellblock H. He is carrying a shank made out of a sharpened piece of metal bracket broken off a metal table. The handle is wrapped in torn sheets. He falls on the female guard and stabs her, not once but many times. He stabs her in the throat and the side of the belly and the back and wherever else his hands can reach. She makes little noise besides a sad grunting. The blood leaves her body and pours onto the ground. When she is good and dead, the man gets up and trots off. He buries the shank in one of the garbage cans lining the yard, not caring if anyone finds it, knowing that it won't matter if they do.

The next day no one can figure how it happened. We all know that the investigation, run by Conroy, will draw a blank. Every few years something like this happens here, and the unsolved murders are shuffled into reports that are soon forgotten in the backs of metal drawers.

The warden sends out a notice to the guards that he knows this is a very old prison. He says he's aware it's almost impossible to count all the inmates at lockdown unless the guards look inside each cell and confirm live heads. He knows with all the budget cuts, they are understaffed, and the idea they can count three thousand every night feels impossible. In the newer prisons, the super-maxes, there are electronic locks and motion sensors. In those horrible places, a man spends his entire life in a metal pod inside one pod inside another, and he never sees the outdoors, smells the sky or dirt, or touches real rock or soil. But our enchanted place is very old. It was built more as a small town of ancient buildings with wood doors and hinged windows and cell door locks easily filled with a wad of chewed paper. The warden writes that having inmates out of their cells after dark is an old problem in our enchanted place, but now a guard has died for it, and it must change.

At least the female guard has the solace of knowing that her body will not go to the oven. They lift it on a real stretcher and take her out to find her family. They empty her locker and take the knitting needles and balls of yarn, and the battered purse that has seen better days, and the wallet stuffed with coupons and pictures of her kids.

Then she vanishes the same way we all do, so I suppose it is not much different.

I hear the soft clop of the lady as she walks past my cell, and I can feel the hot storms that rage inside her. The closer she comes to the priest, the more her insides rebel. She wants this and cannot have it: the peace of being known.

She is afraid if she shares her soul with him, he will reject it. Then she will be lost forever. Then she will be like the men she works with—alone.

I wish I could go to my cell door and call to her.

"Lady," I would tell her, "it will be okay. Go to the priest and ask him. Ask him, Will you know me? See what he says."

I can't say anything to the lady. Even if I could talk, I don't know how to have those conversations. I heard one only once, during that visit with my grandparents. I remember the warm pajamas after the bath and the rich feeling of the cocoa in my belly. I remember curling up in their guest bed under a thick scratchy wool blanket and listening to them talking softly in the room next to me. The talking sounds that came through that wall were not hurting sounds or sad sounds. They were peaceful sounds. That night I got up and touched the walls and put my head on them and listened. Is that what love sounds like? The sound of peace in their voices?

I know that when I read books about love, they are telling the truth. The truth of it winds around my heart and tightens in pain. I try and see it through my eyes, raised to my stone ceiling, and I wonder, What is it like to feel love? What is it like to be known?

The lady is like me in many ways. Serpents crawl inside her. She is deathly afraid that others will see them. She is afraid, and yet she wants the priest to see inside her and accept the monsters that wrap around the secret, pure part of her—the part she managed to save, miraculously, that so many of us have lost. She knows the monsters are there and yet wants to be seen.

Her courage frightens and amazes me. It makes me hopeful for her. It makes me crave happiness for her. Is that what you call love? Is that what you call hope?

The night silk skies, they fail to exist. The dark road is like a ribbon under your car. Gone. The wife waiting for you, even the tiny dimple at the corner of her mouth. Gone. The stars outside—oh, to see them with her once more—and the faint smell of barbecue for the birthday you missed again because you were working late again. Gone.

The warden stands in his backyard. What soon will not be his backyard anymore. He smells the overpowering smell of fir and cedar and the river from afar, of the smoldering ashes of the barbecue of his neighbors—the lazy assholes don't wait for the fire to burn down, they just keep soaking it with fluid, so the burgers must taste like lighter fluid—and the damp loam of the beds his wife once turned over for the fall onions that she grew not so many years ago, and the distant hills, and the faint remembrance of shampoo wafting from the open bathroom window where she once showered.

He knew this grief was coming, and here it is, no different or better or anything. He doesn't want to lie to himself. He doesn't want to tell himself that his wife wanted to leave. He doesn't want to pretend she lived in pain and regret and longed for a place of peace. All of that is bullshit. She didn't want to die. He didn't want her to die. Fuck heaven, he thinks— bring her back.

Bring her back.

The lady visits the home she grew up in. She doesn't know why she came, but here she is, standing out front.

She could never bring anyone here. The yard is pitted with dog turds, and the ancient white siding is stained green-black with mold. The sole window out front is spotted, as if someone inside were spitting on it. Not much has changed, she sees. Probably the same landlord, fleecing the poor of their welfare checks. The limp curtain twitches, and she sees a face—a child's face. It is small and scared but could be her own, back in time.

She decides to move before an angry parent comes out, wondering why there is a lady in a suit standing on the sidewalk, staring at their home. They might assume she is a social worker, come to wreak havoc on their lives.

She walks around the corner, seeing into the backyard. The same laurel hedges are there, capped with the same sliver of sky. She remembers how she used to think that if she prayed hard enough, her dream worlds would come true. She and her mom would wake up one day on the magical island and eat the dripping fruit. Or the best one of all: Her mom would turn around one day with her eyes wide awake, and she would be all there, and she would rush to her and say, Oh, baby.

The attorneys have been calling the lady, and for the first time she doesn't call them right back. She can hear the panic in their messages. The time has passed and the hour is here. If they are going to file with the court, they have to do it now. They ask if she has found anything, if there is any hope at all.

The lady feels silenced. No, not silenced. Quiet. Listening. She sees the path Auntie Beth hobbles along to her porch. She sees the skies over Sawmill Falls. She sees York, real flesh and blood in the Dugdemona cage. Flesh and blood as real as the warden's. As the priest's. As hers.

She wishes she could talk to someone. She imagines talking to the priest.

She has danced with death these years, pulling some bodies from the flames, walking away, and letting others perish.

For the first time, she truly feels it. She feels the pull of life the way the lakes pull their streams into them, mixing the fresh with the cold. Like her mother must have felt with the stirrings in her belly that were knitting joyously into new flesh: her. She wishes she could feel that someday—the creation of new life inside her body. A new being, a water baby born of the blue forests.

She also feels the pull of death. Although she doesn't know about them, she senses the flibber-gibbets waiting near the oven. She feels their implacable gray skins and the coolness and despair of their desire. Will she feed York into their oven? Will she let them steal his last kindling warmth?

Weeks have passed for the white-haired boy, and life is no different or the same.

Summer is here in force, the sky a bright hammered dome over the yard, but the boy doesn't know it. He doesn't feel the dust under his feet or the warm sun on his skin. It doesn't matter to him if it is hot or cold. He gets letters from home, and they are like missives from a foreign land. His mother writes that his sister won the fifth-grade talent show and that she makes his favorite rolls for breakfast every Sunday, the orange kind with icing. She says his grandpa Frank is feeling much better, and their crazy neighbors got drunk on the Fourth and lit the lawn on fire with their stupid illegal fireworks. His dad adds postscripts that he intends to be funny but are not funny, like, *Don't turn into a career criminal, son.* The boy reads the letters and wonders if he ever lived in that world and whether he can go back. He knows the answer: He can never go back.

His days, at least, are predictable. He goes to mess three times a day. He works in the clothing factory, where he gets paid forty cents an hour. He doesn't complain about the work or the slave wages; the time spent at the clothing machines, slicing the blue denim, acts as a salve. It is the only time his brain is asleep. He beds in his cell with the snoring, guttering old man. And twice a week, sometimes more, a big beef will come to him—in the yard, in the mess, in the halls, anywhere they want, it seems—and tell him when or where. Or does it soon after, up in a stairwell or behind a door. The big beefs seem to walk with impunity, anywhere and everywhere, under the smiling sardonic eyes of that intelligence officer Conroy.

He tells himself he will not think about it when it happens. He will blank it out. That never works. He is wide awake and screaming inside through the whole thing. Always. He wonders who made up the lie that people can blank out such things.

Today he sits at lunch mess with the other broken men. He sits next to a thin reedlike man with sandy hair. The man might have been good-looking once, but now his face is lopsided, as if he were badly beaten and had his jaw reset. The man could be nineteen or he could be thirty. The boy realizes he doesn't know the man's name, though they have been sitting next to each other for weeks.

The man begins talking in a low, broken voice, as if he swallowed splinters. He tells the boy he worked as a landscaper. "Till I got sent here for drugs," he says in his whispery, broken voice.

The boy looks at his tray. He thinks it is rice—if rice has round black spots in it, like bugs. There is a pile of damp, rotten shredded iceberg lettuce that smells like fish. The boy thinks of the meals his mother used to make—lasagna and garlic bread, bowls of buttered peas, brownies with homemade white icing, and tumblers of icy cold milk to wash it all down. He remembers coming home from school and filling a mixing bowl with cereal and milk and eating it all. He pushes down those painful memories with force.

"How long have you been here?" the white-haired boy asks the man, tentatively spooning a little of the rice into his mouth. One of the black spots cracks unpleasantly under his teeth, spurting a vile taste in his mouth. His hunger lately is a raging, shaking force, and yet he cannot make himself eat this food.

"Four years," the man whispers. He shows a fearful broken-toothed smile and rubs his pants legs nervously with his hands. The boy feels like scooting a little farther away. "It was supposed to be just one year," the man adds.

"One?" the boy asks softly, looking at his tray.

"Yeah." The man spoons the vermin-filled rice into his broken-toothed mouth, closes his rubbery lips, holds his nose, and swallows hard. "I got an infraction." The man's voice lowers even more, and he tilts his head down so that only he and the boy can hear, though none of the other men at their table listens.

"An infraction?" the boy whispers.

"That guard Conroy, he was behind it," the man whispers, his brown eyes on the boy. "Planted my cell with dope. I got three years on top of the one I already had."

"But—why?" A dawning horror awakens in the white-haired boy. It fills his work boots with terror and gives cold air to the sagging of his pants behind his hollowing thighs.

The man gives a loony, broken smile and says in his husky voice, "I was a favorite—just like you."

The white-haired boy wanders the yard. He wanders the cellblocks. Men take him without recourse or reason. They can see his soul has left and there is nothing to feel bad about anymore. When they are done, the men turn away in disgust, scars on their cheeks showing the battles they have fought—and lost—for the same reasons.

The boy wanders late at night, long past lock-down. The classrooms are in shadows, the win-dowless Cellblock H a dark hole that swallows screams. He wanders through the clothing fac-tory and sees the machines standing shrouded in shadows. He wanders into the mess, the moon-light coming in through the tall cafeteria win-dows, highlighting the tables wiped with smears of gray rag juice. The trash cans are filled to over-flowing with rank food and blood-smeared nap-kins from men with rotten teeth and untreated gum disease.

The boy wanders, and it occurs to him that we have a sun and a sky, a moon and a cloud, a ground and a grave. Before he came here, he thought death was an innocent thing. Now he can see that death is a choice.

When the guards catch him wandering late at night, they sigh and lead him to his cell, where the wheezing old man rises to let him in his bunk. The old man and the guards exchange glances in the dark, the moonlight showing in the old man's rheumy eyes.

No one bothers to demerit the boy for wandering. Usually, this offense would mean a month in the hole and, if caught again, a longer trip to the metal coffins of Cellblock H. Since the female guard died, the guards have become even harsher with the wanderers. But they take pity on the boy. They can see though he is a lost boy, he is a useful boy. Boys like him keep the men peaceable. They keep the men from rioting. The men spend time arguing inside themselves about the boy, whether he represents them or not, whether they want him or not, whether this is a line they should cross. A boy like him keeps the men from thinking about the revolting food, about working for slave wages, about the unfairness of a man like Conroy. One useful boy is like a lightning rod that moves the prison away from storms.

When the boy is at work, he loses himself staring at the sharp blades of the mechanical shears that cut the cloth. Chop, chop, the blades fall, slicing the heavy blue denim as it passes down the line. Farther down the line, other men run the pieces through sewing machines, while still others stamp the cloth with a heavy blue ink badge, turning out the clothes that are currently fashionable with gangbangers and kids who dream of prison life like a romance.

The boy has heard how Risk and his crew make shanks out of these sharp blades and any other item

they can use. He thinks about how such knives—
hundreds of them—are hidden all over the prison,
taped under desks, buried inside mattresses, tucked
in the endless rat holes in the old walls. For a price,
anyone can rent a shank. Anyone but the boy, that
is. If he tried to buy a knife, even to kill himself,
word would get back to Risk.

But he was a handy boy in his dad's workshop.
He looks at the glittering metal blades and thinks, I
can make one.

The only question is, What will I do with it?

He wanders the prison, his eyes unseeing. He
knows the cellblocks where Risk and his cronies
roar with laughter at night, drunk on pruno. He
knows the stairwells where the smell of old blood
drifts from the stone like a cold afterthought. He
knows the quiet hallways of the administration
building where the guards and staff have offices.
The building is locked at night, but the boy knows
there are windows that cock open to the sultry summer nights, and sometimes he drifts under the shadows of those windows, along the dark walls where
the guards in the towers cannot see.

The boy wanders out to the yard. The men turn to
look at him and glance at the rape shed and shake
their heads. The boy just stands there like a ghost,

his white hair hanging in a halo around his vacant face, the red lips standing out like punch, his legs two thin sticks under his pants. The tender belly of youth has disappeared into a hollow cavern under his uniform, and sometimes when he reaches to his privates to piss, he thinks there is nothing there. That little snail shell has just gone up and disappeared.

The boy stands there, swaying. He is watching Risk and his cronies at the weight pile, hearing the slap of metal and the hooting call of a dead lift done well. The men flex their muscles and laugh, and Risk throws back his tangled hair. Risk doesn't see the boy anymore, unless he wants to see him. The boy is no more than a wet carcass to them.

The boy watches Conroy leave the administration building and cross the yard. The men part for him. The tallest trees in the yard sway, and at their center is Risk.

Conroy walks toward Risk with a small, knowing smile. He wants a call on the yes phone, and he knows what to tell Risk. A new shipment of men is coming in. There is a boy on the transport bus, a tender little Hispanic boy of fifteen, a boy with soft velvety skin and fine black hair, a boy so young that he has down on his cheeks. Conroy knows what Risk likes, and he knows how Risk will pay for it.

The white-haired boy watches the dust rise around Conroy's dress shoes as he makes his way to

Risk. He watches the two slap backs and laugh and walk off together. The entire enchanted place sighs.

The heart of the boy holds one last hope. It is an idea so precious, he cannot name it. The idea will not fix things, because nothing can be fixed. The idea will not make him happy or whole, because he will never be happy or whole again.

But this idea—he holds his emaciated hands out in front of himself to see if there is a tremble. There is none.

The boy watches as Risk and Conroy finish their walk and talk with a handshake. Risk unconsciously flexes his shoulders in anticipation. The other men at the weight pile see this and smile with pleasure.

But it is not Risk whom the white-haired boy is watching. It is Conroy, with the black dress shoes and the guileless eyes. It is Conroy, waiting for a call on his yes telephone.

The lady visits York. Her face is drawn. She has not slept.

York is waiting in the Dugdemona cage. His execution date is only a few days away. He is no longer interested in the fraction of sky in the window. He stares at the lady. "So?" he finally asks.

She sees the fear in his dark eyes. He is scared she has come to say she has saved him, that a court date has been set. He is terrified he will be led to the Hall of the Lifers, blinking at the sunlight, to wait endless years for death, unless he is stabbed to death first. He will have to worry about being sent to the metal coffins of Cellblock H, or catching the fury of Risk and his friends. If death row is a sharp punishment, life without parole can be an endless torture.

Death was his safety net. It was the answer to all the inner confusion, to the secret knowledge of the unspeakable harm he caused others. It was his way out of whatever hell he lives in.

She sees this now. She sees it is truly what he wants.

She thinks about how strong the life urge was in her mom, despite all those who would extinguish it, and how that urge gave birth to her. She sees the opposite in York, made of stronger cloth but full of evil, resolved to leave.

Has she made the decision before? She is not sure. She will ruin her career if she does as he asks. She looks at the thick folder in her hands. "I have something for you," she says slowly.

"What?" His voice is quiet.

She rises up, trembling, and slides the folder toward York in the Dugdemona cage.

"I want you to decide."

The lady and York end up talking for hours. Knowing he is barely literate, she gently explains all she has found—the medical records, the interviews, and the abuse. Above all, the blood test.

She tells York that he was born with syphilis. The disease notched his teeth, deformed his bones, and caused the strange fevers and rashes of his early health records. It germinated in his body, traveling up his spinal cord and into his brain, where it hatched into fervid, insane desires. Eventually, it will kill him, just as it killed his mother.

"If this had come up at your trial, you could have been found guilty except for insanity," she explains. When he looks blank, she goes further. "It's possible you would have been sent to a mental hospital. In the least, you would have gotten life without parole." The lady pauses. "That could still happen, if I give this information to the attorneys."

"They would get me a new trial?"

"Yes."

"It's possible I could even get out of here? Live in some mental hospital?"

The lady's eyes are dark with contained fear. She is wondering how high the gates are in the mental hospital, how firm the fence. "Yes."

He brushes the top of the folder and smiles a little. "My life is right here."

"Yes."

"Thank you."

She blinks, surprised. "You're welcome."

He sits in the cage for a long time, just holding the folder. His face is more peaceful than she has ever seen it. Then he looks past her, out the small window to the scrap of sky over her shoulder. The sky is soft blue today, and he thinks he can almost feel the warm sun.

"Here." He passes the folder back to her, and she takes it with careful hands. He leans forward. Their dark eyes meet.

"Let me tell you what I want," he says.

When we have a publicized execution, people line up outside to chant.

On one side are the Advocates. On the other side are the Victims. The warden thinks the Advocates are more like victims of their flagellation, and the Victims are more like advocates for death.

The warden stands at his window and watches them all show up in the blazing sun, each side driving cars blazoned with bumper stickers. They haul signs from their backseats on sticks of wood so fresh, they bleed sap. He thinks these demonstrators are ghouls, like people who leave teddy bears at shrines for dead children. They're into it for the entertainment. After they are done, they will probably go eat pancakes.

Today they line up for York.

Most executions tend to happen without much notice. It is only because York wants to die that his case has gotten so much attention. This irony does not escape the warden.

It is only four in the afternoon, and the sky is a clear eye of heat, but already the two sides are in the parking lot outside the prison. For now they ignore each other. The Advocates wear red ribbons because York said that was his color. Don't they see the joke? The Victims carry signs with pictures of York's victims. The warden hates it when they do that. They didn't know those girls. They don't know their families. They have no right to do that, he thinks. Give those poor girls some peace.

The warden has been in the prison since early morning. Since his wife died, he doesn't want to be home. The once warm ranch feels dead to him. Once it sells, he plans to rent some anonymous place with beige walls and Formica counters and nothing to remind him of what he has lost.

The warden sighs. The day will be long. Execution days are always long. He has to stay in his office because the phone will be ringing off the hook and will ring until the execution at midnight. He sits down heavily at his desk. Sometimes he thinks the death penalty is one big jest. It is like a game where no one wants the killers like York to die. So they give them attorneys like Grim and Reaper, then watch as the game gets played out for decades and the families of the victims wait and suffer.

It is hot as blazes, he thinks. Two fans are running, but nothing moves the sluggish air in his office. When they have heat waves, the inmates drop like flies, and even staff members collapse from heatstroke. Lord, to have air-conditioning. Air-conditioning in the summer and decent heat in the winter—wouldn't that be fine?

The phone rings. It is a call from the chamber. All systems are ready to go. The black shirts are ready.

He catches up on reports and paperwork. He sees Conroy has busted another drug smuggler in the visiting room—good work. He shakes his head at his final report on the dead female guard. Apparently, there was information that she was mixed up with inmate corruption. He's disappointed. He liked her. He reads a report on Cellblock H. He asked a commission to look into the building. The commission found that the inmates needed to be given time out of their cells for their mental health. He nods in agreement and writes some suggestions. If they keep having the problems of suicide and death in Cellblock H, he will shut the place down and start fresh. He is annoyed that he inherited the program.

Any reasonable person can see that locking men down like that is no good.

The warden reads an estimate from a construction firm on the costs of updating the prison with modern locks and motion sensors to keep the wanderers at bay. The price tag gives him a wry smile. He can't wait to see the response from the capitol on that one. It might be as much fun as the time he asked for better food. The hue and cry over how he wanted to pamper prisoners was amazing.

The chanting and singing have started outside. He looks at his watch. Hope you've got good voices, guys, he thinks—you've got hours to go.

At six o'clock he eats his packed dinner. Cold lasagna from the deli. A rather stale piece of focaccia bread. A pat of butter. A can of light lemonade. He finishes with homemade banana-walnut bread taken from the freezer. He takes one bite before it makes him think of his wife, and he puts it down.

He fields two hours of phone calls, all from freaks who somehow got his number. One guy sounds like he is masturbating. Many just scream "murderer" at him before hanging up.

Eight o'clock. The wait is killing me, he thinks ruefully, and laughs despite himself. He doesn't see how his face folds into creases of sadness when he is done.

Dusk is falling. A breeze blows off the river and

comes in his window. It feels good. The sun dips, and the sky illuminates into a deep gray streaked with pink. The geese take flight and pinwheel back to the river.

He calls a guard down on the row. "How is York holding up?"

"Happy as a pig in shit," the guard says.

"Any last-minute visitors? The priest?"

"Says he doesn't want to talk to anyone, least of all that weepy bastard."

"Good." The warden pauses. "You see the lady?"

"Nope. Not for a few days."

This concerns the warden. He tries to reassure himself that it is too late for her to be petitioning the courts. He knows it is never too late.

He gets a mildly hysterical phone call from the prison doctor. They had a problem with the machine, but they worked it out. Yes, they did the practice runs. The chairs for the witnesses are set up. They put out coffee and donuts for the victims' families, who have not yet arrived.

All systems go. Nine o'clock. Three hours to go. The chanting is loud and angry. He is glad he has the state police outside to manage the circus. He doesn't have to worry about the inevitable fights. The victims' families show up. He can always tell when that happens, because the crowd roars in both abuse and support. Armed guards chaperone the families to the viewing room in the chamber. He will see the families when he brings down York, and talk to them after he is dead to make sure they are okay.

The building starts to lock down for execution. One by one the watchtowers flash their lights—the yard is clear. All inmates are supposed to be in their cells. Prison doors slam, and the red lights down the halls and over the towers flash twice. The guards on the rows take their chairs.

The yard is dusty and alone, and in the towers, the guards stand and wait, rifles over their shoulders. It is night now. The stars come out over the yard, and strong lights illuminate the parking lot.

The Advocates cheer. The famous nun has arrived. The Victims frown. They cannot chant against a nun. Their voices grow sulky. They chant louder.

There is a knock on the door. The chief of inmate services, letting him know all is well. The warden says thanks.

Ten o'clock. His phone has grown silent. As each hour passes, the chance of reversal grows slimmer. Unless the lady has done something he doesn't know about. He reminds himself that he has never had a date with death changed so late in the game. But there is a first for everything.

The chanting has taken on a harsh, ringing sound, with the two sides bouncing off each other. At least there aren't news cameras. The public is bored with executions. Still, an armed guard will escort him to his car when it is all done, and one of the state police will check under the hood. A warden in another state was killed when a bomb strapped to his car went off following an execution. The warden thinks, Why do we make it so hard? Why do we make it so easy?

A wind picks up, and a sweet night smell comes in the window. He yawns. He drinks a cup of strong hot coffee from the thermos on his desk, laced with plenty of sugar.

He keeps glancing at the phone and realizes he is waiting for a call about the lady, and he feels a twinge of fear—for her—that she will not win this case. He shakes his head at himself. He is in the wrong business when he starts rooting for the lady. He tells himself she makes his life interesting.

Eleven o'clock. Time to go get York. He will meet the black shirts, and they will walk York to the chamber. The warden will watch as the doctor threads his arms to the medical vine, and he will ask York his last words, and he will press the buttons and watch York die. He will hear the time of death, and hear the cheering and the veneration

outside, just like all the other executions he has
done, including those of Striker and the ones who
came before. He will comfort the families and talk
to any guards who regretted putting on the black
shirt—there is always one, a wet-eyed man who
felt sick at the taking of a life. The warden respects
those men as much as the others. This is just a job,
he tells them, and there is no value in doing what
you don't want to do. Then he will go home to his
empty house, with the overgrown lawn and the
For Sale sign outside, and remember his dead wife.

They are singing outside. Lord help him, it is
"Kumbaya."

Time to go. He gets up heavily.

Down on our row, York has been waiting at his door
for hours.

He finished his last meal with gusto, exclaim-
ing loudly for everyone to hear that he hasn't had
an appetite in ages, but boy howdy, this was good.
I could smell the fried chicken from where I was—
fried chicken and mashed potatoes with gravy, corn
on the cob, and hot apple pie.

York didn't trust the kitchen to make his last
meal, so he ordered out. A guard brought the last
meal in a huge grease-spotted bag from Kentucky
Fried Chicken. I remembered hearing about the

place when I was a kid; I never ate there, but it sure smelled good. York crunched through the chicken skin so loudly that everyone could hear it down the row. My mouth was drooling. Some of the men were groaning, and York was laughing through a mouthful of food. I looked at my own dinner tray. There was the gray-green mush in a dishwater puddle, and a circle of something that might have been brown lentils but could have been mouse turds. On the side was a small glass of greenish instant milk in a dirty paper cup with bloody tooth marks from a previous drinker. I scraped a dot of blood off the wax rim, thinking about the priest. He left hours ago, after being turned down by York for prayer, shaking his head at the jubilation coming from York's cell.

I have never heard York so happy. He is waiting and laughing like a young boy at his cell door, exchanging jokes with the other men on the row, eagerly counting down the minutes until his own death.

"Can't wait, buddy," he says, dancing off the bars. "Going to be sweet."

"Going to meet your Maker, York?" one of the men calls.

"Hell, yes. Out of this place."

"Blessed relief, brother. Blessed relief."

The door slams at the far end of the row. Everyone breathes and sighs.

THE ENCHANTED   239

Everyone knows the gait of the warden, followed
by the black shirts. Silence follows their footsteps.

The warden reaches York's cell. The black shirts
are behind him.

York looks past the warden as if he expects to see
the lady standing there, waiting with his folder. But
she is gone.

He smiles, relieved. "I'm ready, boss."

The warden swings the keys, and the guards go
to open the cell.

And that is when we all hear the faintest trembling,
the tiniest tremors that tell us the horses are getting
ready to run again. I stand up off my cot and go to
the back wall. I press my hands on it and feel the
horses tremble through the stone, feel the way the
vibration moves down my thin legs with the spaces
between the thighs, feel it in the knobby bones of
my knees and the curving cradle of my bony hips.

I spread my fingers and I feel the golden horses.
They are deep below me, snorting, wild-eyed with
expectation. They roll their dark eyes, and hot
steam billows from their mouths like streams of
gold froth. The hot yellow mist rises all the way to
my cave. What are they excited about? The ground
shakes a little in response. Something big, they say.
Something big is happening this way right now.

The guards are shouting in the halls, "Get down,

get down," as the entire prison begins to shake. The horses are running! Get down, assholes! The warden and everyone fall to the ground as if in prayer.

The horses are running, I think. Run, horses, run!

Sure enough, they answer me, pummeling up closer to the earth, their delighted hooves hammering the underground as they run, their molten bodies channeling their golden heat to the surface.

Far across the yard, deep in this enchanted night, the white-haired boy is out alone. He has been wandering the halls for hours, unmolested, looking at all the men sitting on their bunks, waiting for the execution. He passed the corpse valets, sitting awake at the edges of their bunks, waiting for the calls. On this night of all nights, the prison is empty and quiet. He passes the dark mess, the empty cafeteria tables, the shining scuffed metal cabinets and huge mixing bowls that clatter with the passing tremors. He wanders through closed factories and down empty halls until he comes to a door leading to the yard.

The yard is oh so quiet; there is only the boy. He walks in the shadows under the overhanging buildings so the watching guards do not spot him. The empty picnic tables cast deep shadows, the baseball diamond an empty spot worshipping three bases and a final destination. The blank walls of

Building H loom above him. The oven is waiting. A freshly hired guard has joined the other man in the sweltering lunchroom, not understanding why his coworker is so quiet and withdrawn while they wait for the last body, which will be York. They feel the latest tremors and look at each other in concern, holding the small lunch table as its feet dance on the floor. Down below in the basement, the flibbergibbets pant in expectation, gray clay limbs winding among the ash-caked urns.

The yard dust is so dry, it creaks under the boy's soft steps. His eyes are as pale and unseeing as a blind calf's, and he wanders like one.

The horses are running! I want to yell. Watch out, boy!

The guards in the towers hear the crackle of their radios and drop to the floor as the horses run harder than any of us have ever known. They run so hard, the towers shake. Down in our dungeon, the warden himself is prostrated on his hands on the floor outside of York's cell. All the men are on the floor, the black shirts and guards alike. York begins laughing, and the warden looks at him through the cell bars, both of them with cheeks pressed to the ground, and the warden starts laughing, too.

Only the boy walks, unconcerned, dropping to his hands every now and then from the shaking, only to rise again and make his way, dust on his palms. He is so light that his delicate feet seem to float above the trembling of the horses.

Out in the parking lot, the protestors cry out in alarm and drop to their knees, crawling for the safety of their cars.

Go, horses, I think. Go! And they do, running so hard that the box of my dungeon cell sways from side to side and dust rains down hard from the ceiling. The legs of my cot drum the ground, dancing like water in a hot skillet. I fall to the floor, delighted beyond all measure. Go! And the horses answer, their muscles rising up like golden dragonfly wings fluttering hard beneath my body.

The white-haired boy wanders under the windows of the administration building. His ghostly hair is lifted up. There. One of the counselor windows was left open, cocked for a hopeful breeze and then forgotten. The boy sees his thin hands reach, and then he is pulling himself up, his feet scrambling against the stone.

The office of the counselor is dark. No one is here. The boy lands with soft feet. The lights are off, and the hallways are pitch black. The boy glides down the dark, shaking hall.

Only the office of Conroy shows a light. He has been sitting at his desk, writing reports but mostly tapping on his treasured phone with a pen, lost in thought. He likes to stay for the executions. He likes to feel the circle of life end. Someday he will be the warden and will be the one to watch them die. He will be the one to press the red buttons, the one to make sure the body is tumbled off to the oven, the one to comfort the families of the victims. He smiles to himself as he thinks of this, and he wonders if all men want to be a god, and what is wrong with that?

Conroy has been feeling the horses running. But he doesn't react with wild laughter, like York and the warden, or with joy, like me. He thinks the horses are an annoyance, which is why I think they want to punish him. Yes. They want to punish him.

The horses run around the bend and are trembling next to my wall, and I feel them shaking down the line. York is whooping joyously on the ground, laughing fit to split, and outside his cell, the warden is laughing, too, in the wild abandoned excitement of the moment and the hysterical irony that in this moment of execution, death threatens us all.

"We're all going to die, boss!" York yells, and the warden laughs even harder, clutching the ground and feeling his belly shake against the tremors.

Though the guards in the black shirts and the other inmates listen to the warden in amazement, soon everyone is laughing, splayed like starfish on the floors while the horses buck.

The horses pass, heading straight for the administration building. Their hooves are drumming, the molten gold flowing off their backs, their wild eyes rolled clear back so only the blue whites are visible, so joyous are they in the mindless heat of their run that they do not need to see. The small men with their hammers scamper down the walls to hide, chattering noisily in their excitement.

No one sees the boy, wandering down the dark halls of the offices, his pale hands reaching to guide his way. His eyes are still unseeing.

Go, horses, I think. Go!

In his office, Conroy curses. Damn horses. He wonders if he should crawl under his desk, but that thought seems pretty damn sissy to him. From the time of his infancy, his father taught him about being a man. Men do not fear. Men act.

Another tremor as the horses pass, even closer. He holds his desk. Damn horses. Pens shake in the desk jar, and his phone bounces, the handle rattling. He puts a hand on the black handle to steady it.

The boy sways off the walls down the hallway, and the horses are passing so hard that Conroy is thinking, Maybe I *should* get under that desk.

Instead, he looks up to see the white-haired boy there, swaying like a pale ghost in the shaking doorway. For a moment he can't place the boy, he is so shocked to see an inmate in his door at this hour. It is an unthinkable transgression, a shooting offense. Then he remembers the white-haired boy, remembers he is a broken boy, a used boy, a throwaway boy. It is almost midnight, he thinks, and what the hell is this crazy boy doing in my office?

The boy sways, a ghost in his prison clothes, and it seems odd to Conroy that he is dancing lightly on his feet even as the walls shake. The boy looks at him with wild, lost eyes. Conroy thinks he will have to shoot him. It will be an annoyance, more than anything—he'll have to call the corpse valets, make the death look official. He knows from experience. How many inmates has he shot over the years, from the guard towers, on the yard, in the back of halls no one could see? An even baker's dozen? Fifteen? Twenty?

Conroy stands and reaches for his service holster just as the horses make another joyous pass.

Go, horses, I think. Go! The walls shake, and in my cell, the ceiling is raining dust like a storm, like an avalanche, and I rise to dance in the floating silver cloud. The silver dust is raining in my hair, coating my skin like moth dust. It is coating my arms until they look like the cold beautiful silver skin of fish.

The warden is laughing, more than he has ever laughed, and all of the black shirts are laughing along with him at the absolute crazy joy of this moment, all the men in the dungeon roaring in their cells as the walls are rocking so hard that we think all the walls might come down. Go, horses, go!

Conroy reaches for his pistol, but the horses are there, slipping right under his feet, buckling the very earth he stands on, their muscular haunches heaving and rising to make the earth slip and slide under his black dress shoes.

Damn horses, he thinks, reaching down to catch the edge of his desk just as his legs slip from under him, and he is falling right to the hard floor behind his desk, his knees cracking in pain and surprise.

But it is strange, he thinks. The boy has turned into white liquid, he has turned into *fast*, and pours across the few feet of space like a poem or the wind. The boy moves with uncanny grace, as if the horses are there to help him, as if he knows the spaces between the tremors and this is where his delicate feet touch the floor, so in moments, he is simply There.

He is There and Conroy is fallen.

Only seconds, Conroy thinks, only seconds. His hands are on the floor, and he is trying to get his balance, trying to reach for the pistol at his hip, but the gun feels yards away from his awkward hand, and he can see that the boy's legs are suddenly next to him, along with the uptake of air that says he's raised an arm. A feeling of cold metal—where did that come from? Then he knows. He knows with searing, unending pain as the walls shake and the horses pound and pound and pound and pound, until the floors are awash with the joy of their panting pleasure and the hot beautiful knowledge of a job well done.

The white-haired boy slips back through the dark administration halls as the tremors slowly fade. The walls sigh and creak back into place, the enchantment falling into new rhythms.

In their secret burrows, the little men groom the dust off their jackets, cleaning their small claw hands with tiny narrow tongues and chattering happily.

The warden rises from the ground outside York's cell and dusts off his hands, his sides hurting from the laughter. He looks at York, and their eyes meet. The warden's eyes say, I will make it okay.

The black shirts rise as well, dusting off their executioners' clothes. They open the cell door and offer the manacles to York. He is chained. The men in their cells rise. They come to their cell bars to watch him go.

I don't hear York walk down the hall. I think that is because he is already gone.

In my cell, I rise from the floor, covered in dust, and I wipe my hands across my face to taste it. When I touch my cheeks, I realize I have been crying. My tears taste like salt, like blood, like the inside of a vast ocean.

The white-haired boy drops from the window into the shadows of the yard. He stands in the cafeteria and strips off his blood-spattered clothes, wrapping the bundle tightly around the bloody shank. He buries the damp bundle deep in one of the ripe cans of rotten trash. With luck, the trash will be carried out before dawn, when the trusties wheel the cans to the idling garbage trucks before the first mist clears the river.

The boy stands there naked, shivering slightly, the moonlight on his pale slender body. He walks calmly into the dark kitchen. He reaches under a cabinet where he has stowed a new uniform stolen from the intake room days before. When he puts on the clean dry uniform, he feels he has birthed a new skin.

The lights flash on, and the guards in the towers rise, returning to their posts. The radio comes back on and blares from the towers. The protestors in the parking lot limp to their cars and leave. The horses have run back deep underground to the magic place where they live, with towers of marble and rivers of stone. They shake their manes and roll delighted eyes at each other, laughing and nuzzling each other's golden necks.

On the floor behind his desk, the corpse of Conroy lies, the blood running in crisscross patterns as the ground settles. It will be morning before he is found—long after the kitchen trash has lumbered off to the landfill, long after the corpse valets have wheeled the bodies of the day, including York's, across the yard, long after the warden has been escorted to his car across the empty parking lot, strewn with dropped signs from the protestors.

The boy makes his way to his cell, where the old man has been feigning sleep. He rises and lets the boy inside, lifting the small ball of wadded paper in the lock that closes the door. Their cell is coated with fallen dust, and the two men shake out their blankets. The boy crawls into his lower bunk, and the old man looks at him, his eyes large and dark in the night. The old man reaches out to touch the boy, very gently, before he crawls into his top bunk. Within moments he is snoring.

It will be dawn soon, the boy thinks, and a yawn cracks his jaw. Dawn. I have less than two years to go. Maybe twenty months to go, he realizes. It is like waking up. Twenty months is twenty moons. It is twenty birthdays celebrated back to back. It is one rising and the other ending, and it will pass.

Tomorrow, he thinks, I will avoid mess. I will no longer go to the yard. I will stop wandering the prison. I will stay in my cell until the others pass. I will walk carefully in the halls, minding my back and watching at all times. I will no longer go down any dark halls and especially not down any silent stairs.

I will find the places here that are safe for a boy—for a *man*—like me.

Another yawn cracks his jaw. Maybe, he thinks, I will start with the library.

The lady drives to the blue country once again. She doesn't stop to see Auntie Beth. Instead, she goes straight to the location York told her about—the shack where he lived with his mother.

The shack is even smaller than she imagined, with a low buckling roof covered in dead moss. The windows are gutted, the buckled siding wormed with rodent holes. The door hangs on its hinges. An ancient rosebush still lives, bent and thorny, under the solitary window. She fingers a dried curl of hip and wonders if the rose was yellow or red. It is too late in the season to tell.

The lady carefully pushes the door open, in-stinctively ducking in case anything comes flying out. The single room is empty. There are four round scuff marks on the old wood floor where the bed once stood. Cupboards stand empty, their shelves raided by mice. Graffiti on the gouged, crumbling walls—town kids long gone. A mason-jar-lid ashtray is on the floor, filled with butts. The floor is scattered with crushed beer cans. There is the smell of cat urine and maybe something more feral, like bobcat.

She imagines little York, growing the gawky legs of adolescence, sitting in this room by himself for days, eating the wallboard for hunger. Until a seed hatched and traveled up his spine. Thinking of nothing until the nothing became something bad. How many other thoughts—good thoughts—could have come to you instead, she thinks.

She peers through one broken glass frame. The shack is surrounded with an impenetrable tangle of blackberries and rotted fallen trees. There was no escape, no place to run and hide. Down the rutted road is where York waited for the school bus that seldom came.

She closes the door softly behind her as she leaves.

Back in the car, she touches the folder sitting on the passenger seat—York's folder. It's okay, she wants to tell it, as if the folder is York and York is not dead.

She drives back down, out of the area, past the town of Sawmill Falls, past the roads she doesn't want to see again, back to the road she wants to be on, taking her to the emerald lakes. Her heart opens and she breathes.

She parks at the same motel where she stayed before. The Greek owner is out sweeping her porch, her round middle swathed in a faded apron, her iron hair in a kerchief. She doesn't look up as the lady heads down to the lakeshore, carrying the folder.

The lady is alone on the rocky beach. The sun caps each gentle wave. The lake is quiet today. A lone ripple opens up maybe twenty feet from shore, but no fish jumps. She looks around and sees the blue forests rising up, like reassuring arms around her shoulders—embracing her as she wishes someone once embraced York and all the others. You can wish that now, she tells herself. It doesn't undo what they have done.

She walks until she finds a large rock at the lake edge. It is a peaceful spot, cupped with trees. She pries the rock up, satisfied to see the dark gravelly dirt below. When the fall rains come, the lake will rise, and whatever lies underneath this rock will dissolve into smears of words that will fragment until they become nothing but letters and then not even that.

I'm bringing you to a safe place, York, she thinks. The place you always needed—a safe place to dream. To hope.

That's all I want, he told her during their last visit. A place to rest.

She uses her bare hands to deepen the hole. She picks up the folder, smearing it with dirt. She lays the folder in the hole carefully, then tilts the rock back over it. There. York's past is now another secret.

She thinks she might burst out crying—but she doesn't.

She stands carefully, stretching her back. She stands with her arms smeared in dirt, knowing it will take scrubbing to get the dark gritty soil out from under her nails.

She takes a deep breath and looks up at the sky over the clean lake.

I saw you, York. I knew you—who you really were and what you truly wanted.

"Are condolences in order?" the fallen priest asks the lady.

They are walking under the giant trees that circle the outside walls. The priest's face is lowered, his eyes sad and worried. His hands are in his pockets.

The lady has come to pick up paperwork, but really, it is to decide. The attorneys are still calling her. They sound suspicious. Why didn't she ever call them back, even if to say there was nothing? And where is York's file?

The end is upon them.

"No." She shakes her head, her narrow face troubled.

"Why not? You lost York."

"Did I?" She looks tired.

"Odd what happened to that guard, Conroy, on the same night," he says.

"From what I've heard, he had it coming."

He begins to open his mouth.

"Best you don't ask."

There is something she wants to ask him but cannot. "Sometimes I imagine what you looked like in your robes," she suddenly says.

He looks startled.

"But I like you better this way," she continues. "I think I can see you now."

"That wasn't me in those robes."

They walk slowly, each trying to make the walk last longer without letting it on.

"Will I see you again? For your next case?"

She doesn't answer. "Did you ever have to wash your robes?" she asks.

"No." He stops. They are near the front lobby. There is desperate pain and searching and wild hunger in his face. He sees the enchantment now—he sees the enchantment in her.

She doesn't wait for him to answer. "I would have washed them for you," she says.

The lady walks down our row.

I can tell by the sound of her footsteps that this is her last walk. She tells herself she cannot continue this work anymore—not after what she did. If anyone ever found out, she would lose everything. There is something in the muffled clop that says goodbye. I will savor this sound as I have savored all her other sounds.

I touch my chest under my cover. My heart is beating.

If she keeps going far down the row to the chamber, she will find the priest is in his office. He is sitting at his desk, sick with the thought of losing her.

I want the lady to go down there and find the fallen priest. I want her to tell him—tell him what? Tell him she needs him. Say to him, Come with me, priest. Let us know each other together.

I hear her pause. One more step, lady, I think. One more. Go to him. Save yourself, save him. But she is turning. She is uncertain. She doesn't believe she deserves him or anyone or anything ever knowing her. She thinks she will always be alone.

I cannot let this happen. I rush off my cot and find myself at my cell door. It takes so much effort—I cannot do it, but I must. I push my hands out of the bars and feel the shocking slap of the air on the walk.

The lady is turning. She will see me. I wave one skeletal hand in desperation. The lady freezes, seeing me. Our eyes meet. She is the first person to look at me in a lifetime.

She stands rigid. She looks at me and looks at my bony hand gesturing.

Go, lady. I push with my mind. Go, lady. Go to him now. Please—let him know you.

She just stands there, seeing me—seeing *me*—with her eyes. Then she turns and bolts down the hall, toward the priest.

I am shaking. I go back on my cot and hide under the covers. I wonder what retribution will come. Will the monsters under my skin haunt the lady? Will she infect the priest? Will the little men hear and bring their hammers, or the flibber-gibbets writhe in anticipatory celebration? Will the golden horses return to pound an answer on the lady?

The walls are still. The little men do not come. The flibber-gibbets are quiet. The horses are silent. And my heart is filled with peace.

I sit under that cover for an eternity before I decide the lady is strong enough to have seen me. Someday she will see the monsters for what they are and stop questioning herself about why she seeks them. She will stop feeling bad about wanting to make castles for them. Even monsters need peace. Even monsters need a person who truly wants to listen—to *hear*—so that someday we might find the words that are more than boxes. Then maybe we can stop men like me from happening.

The lady has a gift, and I hope she keeps using it. It is the gift of understanding men like me.

The light above me has flicked on and off many times since. Fall is here. I can smell it in the damp shredded leaves on the bottom of the guards' boots, and I can taste it in the odd leavings on my tray: days of spoiled, green-spotted pumpkins cooked into mush. The fall rains are here. I can taste them from the moisture left on my bars from the leather gloves of passing guards. The rain tastes like rivers.

They say that when the warden heard what Conroy was really about—the shackles of fear removed from men's mouths by his death—he ordered an investigation, a real inquiry, and there have been many changes in our enchanted place. Risk and his cronies no longer shout with drunken power from the Hall of the Lifers. Their cells have been stripped of camp stoves and pruno bags and hidden caches of knives. They wait their turn at the weight pile just like everyone else, and they dine on the same wretched food as everyone else.

Their victims—well, some things never change, but the new men are not so harassed. They have a fighting chance.

The white-haired boy walks among others without fear. His head is high, his eyes are clear. He is counting his final months. He has learned to recapture time, which we all want. Everyone can see the clock in his eyes, like a mystical power that shines the minutes, days, weeks, and years ahead. They can see the future in his eyes. It is like a bright dawning light that lets the young man see far from this enchanted place.

The warden comes for me.

He stands outside the door of my cell. Behind him, I see guards, their faces set. They are wearing the black shirts. These are men I have known outside my cell for so many years, farting and talking and laughing and shoving food trays through the slots, but now they are nothing. I feel the hard shield around their hearts. I know they have put the shield there to protect themselves from what they are about to do.

The warden has soft eyes. He is not afraid of me. He is okay with what he is doing. His heart is clean. "Are you ready?" he asks.

My legs feel frozen. I stand up carefully and leave *The White Dawn* on my cot.

I look around my cell. There are no drawings on the walls, no television, no diary on the stone floor. An empty meal tray is left on the floor. I did not order a last meal. I ate the same food I have eaten for so long.

I will go as I have hoped to become: forgotten.

The warden opens the door. I turn and put my hands out so the guards might cuff me. The manacles feel so cold and surprisingly heavy after so long.

Quiet, say the walls. Quiet, says my heart.

Once I am cuffed, I wait, my back to the guards. They finish chaining my legs. The metal cuffs dangle on my ankles. I seem to have shrunk over the years. The warden waits patiently for me to get chained. His eyes are kind and absent. He is thinking of his next day or what he wants for breakfast or something irrelevant. He wants to get this over with. I am glad he is thinking of his tomorrow and not me. I am glad he kept my secret, glad he honored my wishes. It is better this way; better not to enter the maelstrom like York, better not to see myself reflected in the warm eyes of the lady.

The black shirts signal: Time to move on.

Shuffling, I move. This isn't as hard as I thought.

I am out in the open, beyond my door. This hasn't happened in so many years. The stone halls feel hard and bumpy under my paper slippers. The bottoms of my feet hurt. I am not used to the stones, with the lifts and crannies and ragged edges that stick up.

The warden cups one of my arms. It is the first human touch I have felt in many years. It runs like a shock through my system, so much that I feel like fainting.

I am led, shuffling, down the row. The cell York lived in holds a new man. The small men scatter in the walls, and I think they are taking messages to all corners of this place. The other men do not line up at their doors to watch me pass. There are no calls of "hey man" or "hail Odin" or "keep striding." No brother-to-brother calls, no long-distance goodbyes.

The silence echoes down the long walk. I bow my head and listen to the silence, hear the shuffle of my paper slippers on the walk.

We get to the far end of the row, and slowly, we shuffle down past the office that once belonged to the priest. It is empty, but they say a new priest is coming. The warden says the new priest is young and eager and thinks he can change the world. He won't last long.

The fallen priest and the lady are gone. She took the priest away to the sound of rain in the blue forest, to the sound of laughter and lovemaking after dark.

The lady doesn't know it yet, but I have left something for her. It lies on my cot with a last request for the warden. I have asked him to send my copy of *The White Dawn* to her. I wrote a note on the inside jacket, just from me to her, written with that pencil stub. The note for the lady doesn't say much. Just one word.

It isn't far now.

The warden's face relaxes. The hand on my arm is reassuring and firm. I feel the grip of his fingers and marvel at the layers of feeling through my body just from those two dimples of flesh.

Suddenly, we are there. The door is open. The orange room is bare except for the table in the middle. Next to the bed is the machine. My eyes begin to swim a little. I see the milky tubes on the stand, the red buttons.

There is the old black phone on the wall.

I am not worried about the phone. It will not ring.

There is silence beyond the walls. No voices rise in defiance. No one has come to protest. No one has come to celebrate, either. There are some horrors too deep to contemplate. There are some acts that defy redemption or rage. We all just want to close our eyes to them and forget.

In the distance, I hear the sweetest sound of all. It is a bird singing. Maybe it is one of the soft-tufted night birds, come to say goodbye. It is the most beautiful thing I have heard in many years, prettier than bells, and I know this trip was worth it just to hear that sound. It almost hurts my ears, it is so lovely.

The bird trills and then falls silent. I savor the sound like I used to savor the sound of the lady's feet walking past my cell.

The warm reflection on the side of my face reminds me of the window. I raise my head. The heavy black curtains are opened so the audience can see. The witnesses are lined up in folding chairs in the other room.

That's when I see her. Donald's mom. She is sitting to the far right in the watching area, almost shrouded in darkness. She is much older than I remember from my first trial. She is wearing a pink cardigan that has seen better days. Her face is sagging, and her hair is gray. The last time I saw her, I was eighteen. She was a young mother then.

Her face is pale and swollen from crying. She looks like she has been crying for days, for weeks, for years, for decades and forever. Her eyes burn like lanterns toward me.

I hear it once more. The ring of a dial, and her aching, sad, terrified, miserable, pleading voice on the other line. "Donald? Donald? Is that you, Donald?"

I can hear my own voice, answering her. Why could I talk then? Why only in that moment? I can remember her boy next to me, cowering, covered in blood while the white curtain fluttered. Why did I do those terrible things to her child? Why could I talk only then?

Her eyes are painful holes, seeking answers.

The warden touches my arm. Hands press me until I am lying down. The narrow pad feels so much different than the cot I have known all these years. It is a relief to lie down after that long walk. My feet and knees hurt. The hands are pressing me firmly in place, and they are pulling up the canvas straps and cinching me in. One strap goes across my narrow chest, another over my thighs, another over my ankles, and even more cinch my hands and feet in place.

So many straps, and I want to tell them there is no need. I will not fight the vine.

In the reflection of the window, I see a skinny man with graying patchy hair spread like filaments around a gaunt face. That man is me, old before my time.

The warden lays a hand on my arm, a reassuring weight. His fingers are white with black hair on the knuckles.

The entire enchanted place has been locked down. The guards wait in their dark towers, rifles at their shoulders, calm silence around their hearts. The corpse valets wait in their cells. The yard is empty, the weight pile throwing black shadows. Far below us, the golden horses wait next to scorched cliffs, their heads cocked and listening for the falling thud that says another one of us has been taken. The small men have burrowed into their secret hiding places deep in the walls. They sit back on their haunches and hold their hammers in their clawlike hands. The crematorium oven waits, its fire kindled and creaking, and the flibber-gibbets come out to writhe on the basement floors.

The warden and the guards look toward the clock on the wall. Everyone is silent. The phone is silent. We are all silent. I am glad for this reprieve from all the noise inside my head.

I feel a prick. The doctor has inserted the IV. He quickly tapes it to my arm. Everything is happening so quickly. I look to the ceiling. There is a stain there. Which cellblock is that? Already I am losing my knowledge of this place, it is flowing from me like water. I want to turn and ask the warden, but I am afraid that even if I can speak at this last moment, he will say there are no cellblocks up there, and you've been wrong about everything you have ever thought or said or imagined. No, I will say, I knew this would happen, and it did. I didn't imagine the milky tubes or the little men or that face burning toward me through the glass.

The warden is there above me. His face looks wrinkled and pouched. He is asking me something. "Do you have any last words, Arden?"

I shake my head. There never were any words for me.

The warden looks at the clock, and we all watch the last moments of my life drain away. This is interesting, I think. I know exactly when I will die. Someone is counting. The numbers become a jumble because I am waiting for that word, and it comes now. I watch as the warden presses the button.

ARMED.

"Ready?" the warden asks the doctor, who is watching the machine.

The last moments drain away. "Okay," says the doctor.

The warden touches my arm. "Goodbye, Arden," he says.

Goodbye, Warden.

The warden pushes the next button.

START.

The medicine is flowing. Everyone in the room straightens and sighs with relief, as if this is already over.

I turn my face to see Donald's mom once more, to give her the pleasure of watching the life leave my eyes. I can see her eyes through the glass, burrowing into me, sending her hate into the medical vine strapped to my arm.

I want to tell her to pretend it never happened, that what I did to her son never happened. She should tell herself he died of leukemia or a tragic accident or any of the ways that children can die and their parents can pick themselves up and grieve and move on, their hearts full of hurt but healable. Not of what I did. No one ever heals from what I did. I want her to pretend that I never happened—I was an abortion that went undone. I want to tell her I wish I could take it all back, fold back into the womb, erase myself into a seed, make myself obsolete. Never have been, never was here, never did those terrible, horrible, heartbreaking things to her son.

The phone breaks, and the dial tone starts. "Donald? Is that you?"

She is crying. I can see the tears on her swollen cheeks.

FINISH.

The medicine has started, and it is taking me higher. I feel my body relax. A yawn breaks my jaw. The warden's eyes relax, and he lifts his hand off my arm so I can leave.

I can feel myself rising. My whole body is rising off the table and floating up through the air. I float through the ceiling and through walls and ceiling after ceiling as if the stones are dust and my body is spinning and rising and tumbling out of the room with the air.

Her eyes are following me as I float up higher and higher, and I am through the roof and above all the cellblocks and oh my, there is *air* out here. There is cold air and the flicker of moonlit stars. The air is so cold and so sweet that it hurts my lungs as I start to tumble through the darkness. I am tumbling up through the stars, and down below I can see the little room and her face turned up toward me, and around that I can see the guard towers and the walls and all the cellblocks.

I can see the row below and the men buried inside it, and I can see outside the prison walls. I can see the cold river that runs next to the place and the dark masses of the bushes. I can see the ribbon of the freeway and the roads that branch out like veins, dotted with lights, and I know these lights are the houses where people live.

I am going higher and higher, the walls and guard towers are getting smaller, and I see that the prison is set along fields and dark woods. I can smell fir and cedar and the night wind. I can see the river that connects to larger, darker rivers, and the smell of forests and clouds and stars and the rain and of fish to be born. The homes below string out like centers of pulsing warmth in a black canvas.

I am so high that I can see over the hills and into the mountains. A whole world stretches beyond this place: a world where life runs like steam engines and love crackles like leaves frosted with the dawn. A world where mothers lie with babies on flowered cotton sheets in the afternoon, where men hold their wives and put their faces against the cleft of life.

Just before I get too high, I see one little cabin tucked on the side of a blue-forested hill that overlooks a series of deep emerald lakes.

It is the cabin where the fallen priest and the lady live. He sleeps with her and says her name to her deep in the middle of the night, says it while he comes over and over into her. On this night, they are blissfully unaware of all that is happening. They stopped reading the newspapers months ago, stopped immersing themselves in the pain of others. They are going to decide what they want to do next. They do not see me high above them, tumbling in the night sky. They are curled in a white bed under a steep eave, readying for sleep, and he is raising his face to watch her drift away. He is seeing her as if for the first time, how relaxed she looks, as if her entire body has found forgiveness from pain.

She is murmuring something, a word that sounds like the most precious word of all, after someone's name, and that word is the same as the one I wrote to her on the inside of my book: Love.

I look over past them and shoot like a diamond to see once again the walls that contained me.

Oh, this enchanted place.

This enchanted world.

Acknowledgments

The author would like to thank the following: Luppi, Dontonio, and Markel Denfeld Redden; Richard Pine; Gail Winston; Kirsty Dunseath; Maya Ziv; Eliza Rothstein; Bill Hamilton; Nathaniel Jacks; Victoria Schoening; Ellen Rogers; Lane Borg; the staff of the Metropolitan Public Defenders Office; Bob and Laura Hicks; Stephanie Hunter; Mary Ellen Haugh Rubick; Nancy and Steve Rawley; Julie Shaw; Jimmy Scoville; Todd Grimson; Louis Pain; Randy and Amy Christensen; the performing arts communities of Portland and Ashland; Gary Norman; Deborah Lee-Thornby; Katherine Dunn; Edward Taub; Shirley Kishiyama; Marty Hughley; and most especially, her clients.

About the Author

Rene Denfeld is an internationally bestselling author, journalist, mitigation specialist, and fact investigator in death penalty cases. She has written for the *New York Times Magazine*, the *Oregonian*, and the *Philadelphia Inquirer*, and is the author of four books, including the international bestseller *The New Victorians: A Young Woman's Challenge to the Old Feminist Order*; *Kill the Body, the Head Will Fall*; and *All God's Children: Inside the Dark and Violent World of Street Families*.

Don't Miss These Indie Bookseller Favorites!

Moonglow	The Queen of the Tearling	Magpie Murders	The Free
Michael Chabon	Erika Johansen	Anthony Horowitz	Willy Vlautin

OLIVE EDITIONS for $10 EACH

Available for a Limited Time Only

Commonwealth	The Enchanted	The Golem and the Jinni	Future Home of the Living God
Ann Patchett	Rene Denfeld	Helene Wecker	Louise Erdrich